Anonymous

Our President from the Atlantic to the Pacific

Anonymous

Our President from the Atlantic to the Pacific

ISBN/EAN: 9783337401801

Printed in Europe, USA, Canada, Australia, Japan

Cover: Foto ©Andreas Hilbeck / pixelio.de

More available books at **www.hansebooks.com**

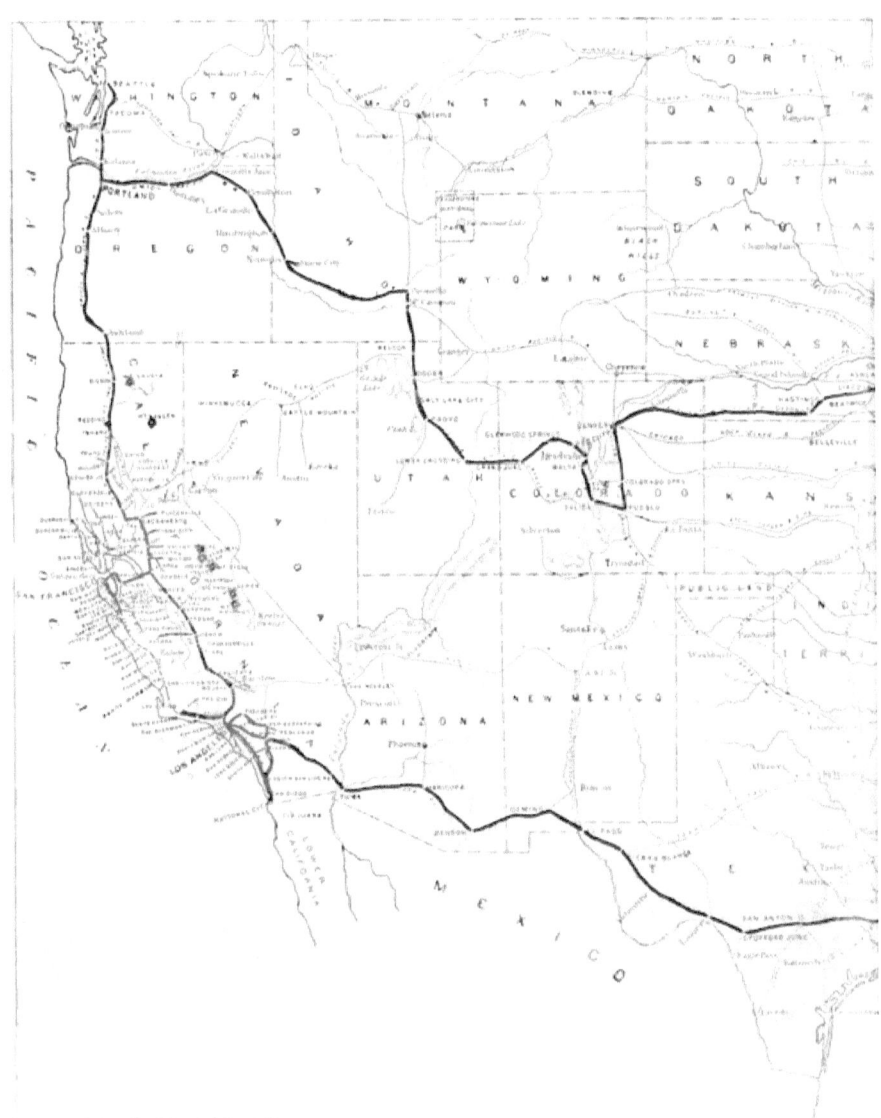

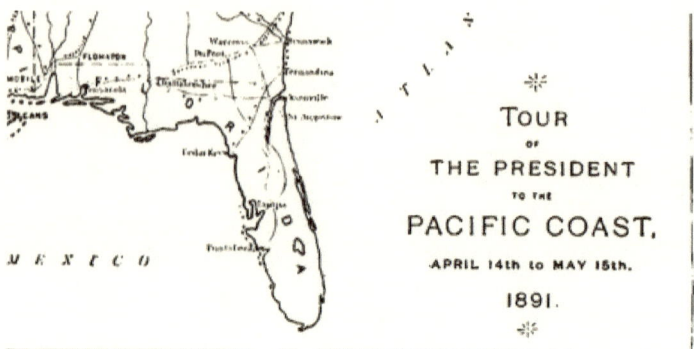

TOUR
OF
THE PRESIDENT
TO THE
PACIFIC COAST,
APRIL 14th to MAY 15th.
1891.

OUR PRESIDENT

FROM THE ATLANTIC TO THE PACIFIC

———————

1891

PRINTED AND ELECTROTYPED BY
HUDSON-KIMBERLY PUB. CO.

To

Mrs. Benj. Harrison

To whom a soverign people have accorded the title of
" The First Lady of the Land," and who so gracefully,
yet with simplicity, fills her exalted position—typical
of the noble wives and mothers of this the most favored
of lands—this volume is respectfully dedicated.

INTRODUCTORY.

A presidential outing appeals strongly to American patriotism. The recent tour of President Harrison from the Atlantic to the Gulf and the Pacific evoked such genuine enthusiasm throughout the entire country, covered, that cities vied with each other to make their welcomes warmer—their receptions memorable days—and a peace loving people laid flowers and garlands in bewildering profusion at the feet of the Chief Magistrate; children showered roses upon him, while fathers and mothers testified by word and action their profound respect for the Man and the President.

To this generous and spontaneous outpouring of personal and public good will, Mr. Harrison responded in many thoughtful, considerate and timely speeches, worthy of a President and a Statesman.

Within thirty days one hundred and forty speeches and short addresses were made by Mr. Harrison and this tax upon the mental resources and endurance of the

President is probably without a parallel in the history of any of his predecessors.

The principal speeches delivered are contained in this little volume and are largely gleaned from the reports published by the Daily Press throughout the section visited.

The presidential party, consisting of the President and Mrs. Harrison, Mrs. McKee, Mrs. Dimmick, Mr. and Mrs. Russell Harrison, Postmaster-General Wanamaker, Secretary Rusk, Marshal Ransdell, Mr. and Mrs. George W. Boyd, E. F. Tibbott, the President's stenographer, Major Sanger, of the army, and representatives of the press associations, left Washington at midnight April 14th and returned on schedule time, May 15th.

KANSAS CITY, June, 1891.

INDEX.

OUR PRESIDENT

FROM THE ATLANTIC TO THE PACIFIC.

ROANOKE, VIRGINIA.
APRIL 14.

The Presidential train arrived at this thriving town at 8:50 this morning, having made the run from Washington on exact schedule time. There were no special incidents on the route. The reception at Roanoke was most enthusiastic. The President shook hands with many hundred people from the rear platform, and in response to repeated demands, made a short speech. The entire population of the place seemed to have gathered at the station, and as many of them as could do so embraced the opportunity to shake hands with the President.

The President spoke as follows:

My Fellow Citizens:—I desire to thank you for this friendly greeting. The State of Virginia is, for personal reasons, entitled, I think, to be placed high in the roll of our states for its great history and the contributions it has made to the history of the whole nation.

For personal reasons I can never fail in affection for the state of my father. I am glad to be here this morning to congratulate you upon the marvelous development which is going to lead the great commonwealth. You not only have an illustrious start behind you, but you have before you prospects of development in material growth, in wealth and prosperity and all that makes a great state such as could never have entered into the imagination of those who laid the foundation of this great commonwealth. [Applause.] I think all of you are aroused now to the realization of the benefits of diversified industries.

In the olden times Virginia was a plantation state. I hope she may never cease to have agriculture for the foundation of statehood, but I rejoice with you that she has added to agriculture the production of coal, the development of iron, and by combining iron and coal is now working products that enter into all the uses of life.

It is out of this bringing together these diversified industries that you are achieving a great growth, as is wonderfully illustrated in what I see about me here today, and have a future which none of us can fully realize. In all of these things we have a common interest. [Applause.]

I beg to assure you this beautiful morning, person-

ally and officially, that in everything that tends to promote the stability of your government, the social order
of your people, the development and increased prosperity
of the state of Virginia that I am in hearty sympathy
with you.   [Applause and prolonged and loud cheering.]

BRISTOL, TENNESSEE.

APRIL 14.

At 2 p. m. Mr. Harrison was escorted to a
convenient place overlooking the Front Street
park and was introduced by Judge W. B. Wood.
In a firm, clear voice which characterizes his
delivery, he addressed the immense concourse as
follows :

My Fellow Citizens:—I have found not only pleasure, but instruction, in riding to-day through a portion
of the state of Virginia that is feeling in a very striking
way the impulse of a new development.   It is extremely
gratifying to notice that those hidden sources of wealth
which were so long unobserved and so long unused are
now being found; and that these regions, once so retired,
occupied by a pastoral people having difficult access to
the centers of manufacturing and of commerce.   In the
early settlement of this country the emigrants poured
over the Alleghanies and the Blue Ridge like waters over

an obstructing ledge, seeking the fertile and attractive
farm regions of the great west. They passed unobserved
these marvelous hidden stores of wealth which are now
being brought into use. Having filled those great basins
of the west, they are now turning back to Virginia and
West Virginia and Tennessee to bring about a development and production for which the time is ripe, and
which will surprise the world. [Cheers.] It has not been
long since every implement of iron, domestic, agricultural and mechanical was made for you in other states.
The iron point of the wooden mold-board plow with
which the early farmers here turned the soil, came from
distant states.   But now Virginia and Tennessee are
stirring their energies to participate, in a large degree, in
mechanical productions and in the great awakening of
American commerce and American influence which will
lift the country to a position among the nations of the
world never before attained. [Cheers.]   What hinders
us, secure in the market of our own great population,
from successful competition in the markets of the world?
What hinders that our people, possessing every element
of material wealth and endowed with inventive genius
and energy unsurpassed, shall again have upon the seas
a merchant marine flying the flag of our country and
carrying its commerce into every sea and every port?

I am glad to stand for this moment among you, glad
to express my sympathy with you in every enterprise
that tends to develop your states and local communities;

glad to stand with you upon the same common platform of respect to the constitution and the law, differing in our policies as to what the law should be, but pledged with a common devotion to obedience to the law, as the majority shall by their expressions make it.

I shall carry away from here a new impulse as a citizen with you of a country whose greatness is only dawning. And may I now express the pleasure I shall have in every good that can come to you as a community and to each of you as individuals. May peace, prosperity and social order dwell in all your communities and the fear and love of God in every home. [Cheers.]

KNOXVILLE, TENNESSEE.

APRIL 14.

The President and party were escorted through the almost impassable crowd to the carriages in waiting, and were driven to the highest point on Fort Sanders.

Alighting from their carriages, the majority of the party made a cursory inspection of the famous battlefield by the light of the fast-fading day.

Carriages were again entered and the party were driven to the Hattie House, from the bal-

cony of which the President was introduced to
a vast audience by Col. W. A. Henderson.

PRESIDENT HARRISON'S SPEECH.

Fellow Citizens:—It gives me great pleasure to
visit this historical city, a city that has given to the country many men who have been eminent in its counsels,
and have brought to the nation they served and to the people who called them into public service imperishable hon-
or. I am glad to visit East Tennessee, the scene of that
early immigration and of those early settlements by men
whose vigor of intellect, strength of heart and devotion
to representative principles were among the most conspicuous of the early pioneers of the West and South-
west. I am glad to know that those traditions of liberty,
that devotion to the cause of the Union which manifested itself in the early contributions of Tennessee to
the armies that went forth from the homes of the Northwest and North, like the steel in these valleys shed its
glorious luster over the hill-tops of the Alleghanies.

You are feeling now a material development that has
become characteristic of all the states. I beg to say to
you that whoever supposes that there is anywhere in the
Northern States any jealousy of this great material progress in the South, wholly misconceives the friendly heart
of the people of the North. This is my wish, as I am
sure it is that of all with whom I associate in political
life, that the streams of prosperity in the South may run

bank-full with any and everything that may promote the prosperity of the State, the security and comfort of the community and the happiness of the individual home, your blesssings may be full and unstinted.

We live in a government of law; the compact of our organization is that a majority of our people, taking those majorities which are prescribed by the constitution and the law, shall determine our public policies and choose our rulers. That is our solemn compact. It cannot be safely broken. We may safely differ about policies, we may safely differ upon the question of what should be the law, but when the law is once enacted no community can divide upon the question of implicit obedience to the law. It is the one rule of conduct for us all. I may not choose, as President, what laws I will enforce, and the citizen may not choose what laws he will obey. Upon this broad principle our institutions rest.

Therefore, all my appeal everywhere I look into the faces of my fellow citizens, is to hold up in veneration and reverence the law of the United States and of the State where you reside, each in its appropriate sphere. We have no other king, we bow the knee to no potentate. Public officers are your servants, but in the august and majestic presence of the law we all uncover and bend the knee.

May every prosperity attend you; may this ground, made memorable by one of the most gallant assaults and by one of the most successful defenses in the history of

the war, never again be stained by blood, but our people
in one common love of one flag and one constitution, in
a common and all-pervading fealty to the principles of
our government, come on to join in weal, in social development, and piety—in everything that makes a nation
great and the people happy; all that the Lord has in
His mind for a nation that He has conspicuously blessed.

JOHNSON CITY, TENNESSEE.

APRIL 14.

There were about three thousand persons, including many Grand Army men, gathered
around a gaily decorated stand in the public
square.

Representative Taylor introduced the Presidential visitors to the people, when the President spoke as follows:

My Fellow Citizens:—The office of President of
the United States, if one of very high honor, is also one
of very high responsibility. No man having conscientiously at heart the good of the whole people, whose interests are under the law in some degree committed to
himself, can fail to feel a most oppressive sense of inade-
quacy when he comes to the discharge of these high
functions. Elected under a system of government which

gives to the majority of our people expressing their wishes through constitutional methods the right to choose their public servants, when he has taken the oath that inducts him into office he becomes the servant of all the people, and while he may pursue the advocacy of those measures to which the people have given their approval, he should always act and speak with a reserve and a respect for the opinions of others that shall not alienate him from the good will of his fellow-citizens without regard to political belief. I shall not speak of what has been done. I have a supreme regard for the honor of the nation, a profound respect for the constitution, and a most sincere desire to meet the great expectations of my fellow citizens. I am not one of those who believe that the good of any class can be permanently and largely attained except upon lines which promote the good of all our people. I rejoice in the union of the States. I rejoice to stand here in East Tennessee among a people who so conspicuously, and at such sacrifice, during the hour of the nation's peril stood by the flag, and adhered to their convictions of public duty (cheers), and I am especially glad to be able to say that those who following other views of duty took sides against us in that struggle, without division in voice or heart, to-day praise Almighty God that He preserved us one nation. There is no man, whatever his views upon the questions that then divided us, but in view of the marvelous benefits which are disseminating themselves over these States, must also bless

God to-day that slavery no longer exists, and that the union of the States is indissoluble. (Cheers.) What is it that has stirred up the pulses of this great region, that has kindled these furnace fires, that has converted these retired and isolated farms upon which you and your ancestors dwelt into busy marts of trade and mechanical pursuits, bringing the market close to the door of the farmer and bringing prosperity into every home? It is that we have no line of division between the States. It is that those impulses of freedom and enterprise once limited in their operations are now common to all the states. We have a common heritage. The Confederate soldier has a full, honorable and ungrudged participation in all the benefits of a great and just government, I do not doubt but that these same men would follow the starry flag if assailed from any quarter. (Cheers.) Now all my fellow countrymen, I can pause but a moment with you. It does me good to look into your faces, to receive these evidences of your good will. I hope I may have the guidance and courage in such time as remains to me in public life conscientiously to serve the public good and common glory of our beloved country. [Cheers.]

JONESBORO, TENNESSEE.
APRIL. 14.

The President made an address from the rear platform of the train.

The President said:

The Scripture speaks, I think—my Postmaster-Gen eral is near, and if I fall into error will correct me [laughter]—of a time when the old things shall pass away and all things shall become new. Tennessee is realizing that beatitude, and steep mountain roads have passed away and the steam-car has come. The old times of isolation in these valleys, when these pioneers, some of whom I see, made their frontier home, have passed away and influences from the outside have come. Life has been made easier to men and easier to the toiling women who used to carry the water from the spring at the bottom of the hill in a piggin, but now by modern appliances have it brought into the kitchen. You have come to know now that not only the surface of the soil has wealth in it, but that under the surface there are vast sources of wealth to gladden the homes of your people, and to bring with new industries a thrifty population. But of all these old things that have passed away and the new ones that have come, I am sure you are exultingly glad in this region, where there was so much martyrdom for the flag, so much exile, so much suffering, that the one Union, the one Constitution, and the one Flag might be preserved,

to know that those old strifes have passed away, and that
a period of fraternity has come, when all men are for
the Flag, and all for the Constitution, when it has been forever erased from the minds of the people that this Union
can be dissolved or this Constitution overthrown.   [Great
cheering.]   On all these new things I congratulate the
people of Tennessee.   Turn your faces to the morning,
for the sun is lighting the hill-tops; there is coming to
our country a great growth, an extraordinary development, and you are to be full participants in it all.   We
have here prodigious resources that are yet to be touched
by the finger of development, and we have the power, if
we will, to put our flag again upon the sea and to share
in a world's commerce.   [Cheers.]

GREENEVILLE, TENNESSEE.

APRIL 14.

The home of Andrew Johnson was specially
cordial in its welcome to the Presidential party,
a feature being the display of flags.

The President said:

I rejoice to see in the hands of the children here that
banner of glory which is the symbol of our greatness and
the promise of our security.   I am glad that by the common consent of all our people, without any regard to past
differences, we have once and forever struck hands upon

the proposition that there shall be one flag and one constitution. [Great cheering.] This city has given to the
country a conspicuous illustration in your distinguished
former fellow-citizen, Andrew Johnson, of what free institutions may do, and what an aspiring young man may
do against all adverse conditions in life.

MORRISTOWN, TENNESSEE.

APRIL 14.

At Morristown, the patriotic people of that
live town and of Hamblen, Cocke, Grainger and
Jefferson counties had assembled in vast numbers, and were enthusiastic to a high degree.

The President spoke as follows :

My Fellow Citizens:—It will not be possible for
me to speak to you for more than a moment, and yet I
cannot refuse, in justice to my own feelings, to express
my deep appreciation of your cordial reception. I visit
to-day for the first time East Tennessee, but yet it is a
region in which I have always felt a profound interest,
and for whose people I have always entertained a most
sincere respect. It seems to be true in the history of
man that those who are called to dwell among mountain
peaks, where the convulsions of nature have lifted the
rocks toward the sky, have always been characterized by

a personal independence of character, by a devotion to liberty and by courage in defense of their rights and their homes.   The legends that cluster about the mountain peaks of Scotland, and the patriotic devotion that makes venerable the passes of Switzerland, have been fulfilled in the mountains of East Tennessee.   In those periods of a great struggle, when communications were difficult and often interrupted, the hearts of the people of Indiana went out to these beleaguered friends of the Union beyond the Cumberland Gap.   I am glad to know that it is not as difficult to reach you for succor, or for friendly exchange, or social intercourse as it was in those troublous times.   Some one mentioned just now that it was only four hours and a half from Chattanooga to Atlanta. That is not my recollection.   (Laughter.)   I think we spent nearly as many months getting there.   (Laughter.)   Travel has been quickened and made easy.   I am glad to know now, by the consent of all our people, without regard to the differences that separated you then, that your highways are open to us all without prejudice, that your hearts are true to the Union and the Constitution, and that the high sense of public duty which then characterized you still abides among your people.   May your valleys always be full of prosperity, your homes the abode of affection, and of all that makes the American home the best of all homes and the sure nursery of good citizens.   (Cheers.)

When he had finished speaking an old gray-headed man stepped up to the platform and reached out his hand:

"Mr. President, I was with you on that trip to Atlanta. I was on the other side, and I want to take you by the hand." The President gave him a hearty shake, and the little scene brought forth rounds of applause. A large number of old ex-Confederates witnessed the scene.

CHATTANOOGA, TENNESSEE.

APRIL 15.

When the Presidential train arrived, fully three thousand people were assembled at the station. The streets of the city were crowded, surrounding towns liberally contributing to the throng. The gaily decorated electric cars rapidly conveyed the party to the incline at the foot of historic Lookout Mountain.

The party remained a few moments on the mountain, as the day was especially desirable for a grand view. With few exceptions the business houses along the line of the President's

route were handsomely decorated, flags and
bunting floating from every window, and drawn
up in line upon McCallie Avenue, the main res-
idence street, were thousands of school-children,
waving flags as a welcome.

President Harrison was introduced by Hon.
H. Clay Evans, and was greeted by deafening
cheers.

The President said:

My Fellow Citizens:—I have greatly enjoyed the opportunity of seeing Chattanooga again. I saw it last
as the camp of a great army. Its only industries were
military, its stores were munitions of war, its pleasant
hill-tops were torn with rifle-pits, its civic population the
attendants of an army campaign. I see it to-day a great
city, a prosperous city. To-day I see these hill-tops, then
bristling with guns, crowned with happy homes; I see
these streets, through which the worn veterans of many
campaigns then marched, made glad with the presence
of happy children. Everything is changed.

The wand of an enchantress has touched these hills,
and old Lookout, that frowned over the valley from
which the plow had been withdrawn, now looks upon
the peaceful industries of country life. All things are
changed, except that the flag that then floated over Chattanooga floats here still. [Cheers.] It has passed from

the hands of the veterans who bore it to victory in battle into the hands of the children, who lift it as an emblem of peace. [Cheers.] Then Chattanooga was war's gateway to the South; now it is the gateway to peace, commerce and prosperity. [Cheers.]

There have been two conquests—one with arms, the other with the gentle influence of peace—and the last is greater than the first. [Cheers.] The first is only great as it made way for that which followed; and now, one again in our devotion to the constitution and the laws; one again in the determination that the question of the severance of the Federal relations of these states will never again be raised, we have started together upon a career of prosperity and development that has as yet given only the signs of what is to come.

I congratulate Tennessee, I congratulate all those who through this gateway give and receive the interchange of friendly commerce, that there is being wrought throughout our country a unification by commerce, a unification by similarity of institutions that shall in time erase every vestige of difference, and shall make us, not only in contemplation of the law, but in heart and sympathy, one people.

I thank you for your cordial greeting to-day, and hope for the development of the industries of our country and for the settling of our institutions upon the firm base of a respect for the laws. In this glad spring-time, while the gardens are full of blossoms and the fields give the promise of another harvest, and your homes are full of happy children, let us thank God for what He has wrought for us as a people, and each in our place resolutely maintain the great idea upon which everything is builded—the rule of the majority, constitutionally expressed, and the absolute equality of all men before the law. [Cheers.]

The trip from Chattanooga to Atlanta was made over the Western & Atlanta road. There were many historical scenes along the route from Chattanooga to Atlanta. These included the battle fields of Chickamauga, Tunnel Hill, Resaca, Dug Gap, Kenesaw and Peach Tree Creek. Short stops were made at each of these places, and the President shook hands with a large number of people. It was at Resaca that Gen. Harrison led the charge against the Confederate battery, in which he lost nearly half his regiment.

Among other places visited were Ringgold and Dalton.

At Cartersville the President spoke as follow:

CARTERSVILLE, GEORGIA.
APRIL, 15.

My Friends:—I have had great pleasure to-day in passing over some parts of the old route that I took once before under very different and distressing circumstances, to find how easy it is, when we are all agreed, to travel between Chattanooga and Atlanta. I am glad to see the evidences of prosperity that abound through your country, and I wish you in all your relations every human good. [Cheers.]

ATLANTA, GEORGIA.
APRIL 15.

The Presidential party left here this morning for Birmingham, Alabama, by way of the Georgia Pacific Railroad, at 9 o'clock. A great crowd assembled at the station, and loud calls were made for a speech from the President, to which he responded briefly, thanking the people of Atlanta for the cordiality of their reception of him. Postmaster-General Wanamaker also spoke for a few minutes. As the train left the city the Atlanta Artillery, the crack military organization of the city, fired a salute, and the Presidential special was on its way to Birmingham.

The following is the address made by the
President:

My Fellow Citizens:—I desire in parting from you
to give public expression of my satisfaction and enjoyment in the brief visit to Atlanta. I saw this city once
under circumstances of a very unfavorable character. I
didn't think then I would like it, although we were making a great effort to get it. [Laughter.] I am glad after
all these years to see the great prosperity and development that has come to you. I think I am able to understand some of the influences that are at the bottom of it
all, and I am sure I look into the face of a community
that, whatever their differences may have been, however
reviewed the question of the war when it was upon us,
can have but one thought now as to what was best. We
can all say of the confederate soldier, who carried a gun
for what seemed to him to be right, that the Lord knew
better than any of us what was best for the country and
for the world. You are thankful for what he has wrought,
and chiefly for the emancipation. It has opened up to
diversified industries these states that were otherwise
exclusively agricultural, and made it possible for you
not only to raise cotton, but to spin and weave it, and has
made Georgia such a state as it could not have been under the old conditions. I am sure we now have many
common purposes, and as God shall give us the power to
see the truth and the right let us do our duty, and while

exacting all our own rights let us bravely and generously give to every other man his equal rights before the law. [Cheers.]

ANNISTON, ALABAMA.

APRIL 16.

Half the population of the city were in and about the station, while several military companies, a great number of school children and a negro lodge were lined up by the side of the track.

After the Mayor, who had accompanied the party from Atlanta, had introduced the President, addresses of welcome were made by ex-Lieut. Governor McElroy and W. A. Stevens, a colored citizen.

The President, standing, responded as follows:

Gentlemen and Fellow Citizens :—I very much regret that I am able to make so little return for this cordial manifestation of your respect and friendship, and yet, even in these few moments which I am to spend with you, I hope I shall gather and possibly be able to impart some impulse that may be mutually beneficial. I am glad to see the great development which is taking place in the mineral regions of the Southern States. I remember well as a boy, resident upon one of the great tributaries of the Mississippi, how the great agricultural products of these states, the corn and provisions raised upon the fertile acres of the Ohio and Mississippi Valleys, were raised in the South. The South was then essentially a plantation region, producing one or two great staples that found a ready market in the world; but dependent for all its implements of industry and its domestic utensils, even, upon the States of the North. I am glad all this is is changed; that you are realizing the benefits of a diversified agriculture, and that the production upon these farms of these staples which you once bought elsewhere is largely increased, and I am glad that to diversified agriculture you have also added the great mercantile pursuits which have brought into your communities artisans and laborers, who take from adjacent farms the surplus of your fertile lands. [Cheers.]

There has been received in the South since the war not less than $8,000,000,000 for cotton, and while I rejoice in that, I am glad to know that in the mineral region there are nearly 100,000 acres devoted to raising watermelons. [Laughter.] No farmer—certainly no planter in the olden time—would have consented to sell watermelons. You are learning that things that were small and despised have come to be great elements in your commerce. Now your railroads make special provision for the transportation of a crop which, in the aggregate, brings large wealth to your people. I mention this as a good illustration of the changing condition into which you are entering.

You are realizing the benefits of home markets for what you produce, and I am sure you will unite with me in those efforts which we ought to make, not only to fill our own markets with all that this great nation of sixty-five millions needs, but to reach out to other markets which enter into competition with the world for them. [Cheers.] We shall do so, and with all this mechanical and commercial development we shall realize largely that condition of unification of heart and interests to which those who have spoken for you have so eloquently alluded. [Cheers.]

And now, wishing that every expectation of all who are interested in this enterprising young city may be realized, that all your industries may be active and profitable, I add the wish that those gentler and kindlier agencies of the school and church, of a friendly, social life, may always pervade and abide with you as a community. [Cheers.]

BIRMINGHAM, ALABAMA.

APRIL 16.

Booming of cannon and shouting from thousands of throats greeted the appearance of the

President and party on the platform of the train.
A temporary stand had been erected in the station, and to this the President was escorted.
Governor Jones, on behalf of the State, eloquently and feelingly welcomed the President
to Alabama. Mayor Lane spoke in behalf of
the city, to which the President responded as
follows:

Gov. Jones, Mr. Mayor and Fellow Citizens:—The noise
of your industries will not abate, I fear, sufficiently to
enable me to make myself heard by many in this immense throng that has gathered to welcome us. I judge
from what we have seen as we neared your station that
we have here at Birmingham the largest and most enthusiastic concourse of people that has met us since we left
the national capital. [Great and prolonged cheering.]
For all this I am deeply grateful. The rapidity with
which we must pursue this journey will not allow us to
look with any detail into the great enterprises which
cluster about your city, but if we shall only have opportunity to stop for a moment, to look at these friendly
faces and listen to these friendly words we shall carry
away that which will be invaluable, and I trust, by friendly exchange of greetings, may leave something to you
that is worth leaving. [Cheers.]

I have read of the marvelous developments which in

the last few years have been stirring the solitude of these Southern mountains, and I remember to-day that not so many years after the war, when I had resumed my law practice at Indianapolis, I was visited by a gentleman known, I suppose, to all of you, upon professional business. He came to me to pursue a collection claim against a citizen of Indianapolis, but he seemed to be bent more on talking about Birmingham than anything else. [Laughter and cheering.] That man was Col. Powell, one of the early promoters of your city. [Cheers.] I listened to his story of marvelous wealth of iron and coal that was stored in this region, of their nearness to each other and to the limestone necessary for smelting; to his calculations as to cheapness with which iron could be produced here, and his glowing story of the great city that was to be reared, with a great deal of incredulity. I thought he was a visionary, but I have regretted ever since that I did not ask him to pay my fee in town lots in Birmingham. [Laughter and cheers.]

My countrymen, we thought war calamitous, and so it was. Destruction of life and of property was great, sad beyond expression; and yet we can see now that God led us through that Red Sea to development in material prosperity and to fraternity that was not otherwise possible. [Cheers.] Industries that have called to your midst many leading men are always and everywhere concomitants of freedom. Out of all this freedom from the incubus of slavery the South has found a new industrial birth.

Once almost wholly agricultural, you are now not less
fruitful in crops, but you have added all this. [Cheers.]
You have increased your production of cotton, and you
have an added increase in ten years of nearly three hundred per cent to the production of iron. You have produced three-fourths of the cotton crop of the world, and
it has brought you since the war about $8,000,000,000 of
money to enrich your people, but as yet you are spinning
in the South only eight per cent. of it. Why not, with
the help we will give you in New England and the
North, spin it all? [Cheers.] Why not, while supplying
sixty-five millions of people, reach out and take a part
we have not had in the commerce of the world? [Cheers.]
I believe we are now to see a renaissance in American
prosperity, and an upbuilding of your American merchant
marine. I believe that these Southern ports that so
favorably look out with invitations to the states of Central and South America, shall yet see our fleets carrying
the American flag and products of Alabama to the markets of South America. [Great cheering.]   In all this
we are united. We may differ as to methods, but if you
will permit I will give you an illustration to show how
we have been dealing with this shipping question. I
can remember when no wholesale merchant ever sent a
drummer into the field. He said to his customers:
" Come to my store and buy ; " but competition increased.
Enterprising merchants started out men to secure customers, and this fellow merchant was put to the choice

of putting men into the field or going out of business. It seems to me that whatever we may think of the policy of aiding steamships, since every other great nation does it, we must do it or go out of the business; for we have already pretty much gone out. [Cheers.]

I am glad to reciprocate with the very fullness of my heart every fraternal expression that has fallen from the lips of these gentlemen who have addressed me in your behalf. I have not been saved from mistakes; probably I shall not be. I am sure of but one thing: I can declare that I have singly at heart the glory of the American nation and the good of all its people. [Great and prolonged cheering.]

I thank these companies of the State militia, one of whom I recognize as having done me the honor to attend the inaugural ceremonies, for their presence. They are deserving (to the Governor) of your encouragement and that of the State of Alabama; they are the reserved army of the United States. It is our policy not to have a large regular army, but to have a trained military that in any exigency will move to the defense of the country; and if that exigency shall ever arise, which God forbid, I know that you will respond as quickly and readily as any other state. [Cheers.]

The Governor.—You will find all Alabama at your back, sir. [Continued cheering.]

I am glad to know, in addition to all this business, that you are doing, or attending to education and to those

things that conduce to social order. The American home
is one thing we cannot afford to lose out of American
life.   As long as we have pure homes and God fearing,
order-loving fathers and mothers, who rear children that
are given to them, and make these homes abodes of
cleanliness, piety and intelligence, American society and
the Union are safe.   [Great and continued applause.]

TALLAPOOSA, GEORGIA.

APRIL, 16.

A large assemblage of citizens and school
children which had gathered about Tallapoosa
Hotel and the grounds opposite, were made
aware of the approach of the President's train
by the blowing of steam whistles in the " Manufacturing District," and the Trombone Band
playing the "Hornpipe Polka," and as the train
came to a stand the Tallapoosa Brass Band
struck up with " Hail to the Chief."

Mayor Head welcomed the President to
Tallapoosa.

The President spoke as follows:

Fellow Citizens:—This large assemblage of people
from this new and energetic city is very pleasant, and

I thank you for the welcome that it implies. All of these evidences of extending industry are extremely pleasing to me as I observe them; they furnish employment to men; they imply comfortable homes, contented families, a safe social organization, and are the strength of the nation of which we are a part. I am glad to see these enterprises that are taking the ores from the earth and adapting them to the uses of civilization have not been started here unaccompanied by that more important work, the work of gathering the children into the schools and instructing them that they in their turn may be useful men and women. [Applause.]

I am glad to greet these little ones this morning; it is a cheerful sight. We are soon to lay down the work of life and the responsibilities of citizenship. These mothers are soon to quit the ever recurring and never-ending work of the home and give it into new hands. It is of the utmost consequence that these little ones be trained in mind and taught the fear of God and benevolent regard for their fellow man in order that their lives and social relations may be peaceful and happy. We are citizens of one country, having one flag and one destiny. We are starting upon a new era of development, and I hope this development is to keep place and to be the promoting cause of a very perfect unification of our people. [Cheers.]

We have a Government whose principles are very simple and very popular. The whole theory of our institutions is, that pursuing those election methods which we have prescribed under the Constitution, every man shall exercise freely the rights that the suffrage law confides to him, and the majority, which if it has expressed its will, shall conclude the issue for us all. There is no other foundation. This was the enduring base upon which the fathers of our country placed our institutions. Let us always keep them there. Let us press the debate in our campaigns as to what the law should be; but let us keep faith and submit with the deference and respect which is due to the law when once enacted. [Applause.]

The development which is coming to you in these regions of the South is marvellous. In ten years you increased your production of iron about 300 per cent,—nearly a million and a quarter of tons—and you have only begun to open these mines and to put these ores to the process of reduction. Now I want to leave this thought with you: In the old plantations of the South you got everything from somewhere else. Why not make it yourselves? [Cheers.]

MEMPHIS, TENNESSEE.

APRIL 17.

At the Merchants Exchange, fronting on Court Square, which was massed with people, the President was introduced to the assembled crowd by Mayor Clapp, who welcomed him on behalf of the city.

In responding to the welcoming speech the President said:

My Fellow Citizens:—The name of the city of Memphis was familiar to me in my early boyhood. Born and reared upon one of the tributaries of the great river upon which your city is located, these river marts of commerce were the familiar trading points of the farmers of the Ohio Valley. I well remember, when on the shores of my father's farm, the old Broad Horn was loaded from the hay press and the corn crib to market with the plantations along the Lower Mississippi. I remember to have heard from him, and the neighbors who constituted the crew of those pioneer crafts of river navigation, of the perils of these great waters, of the snags and soyers and caving banks of the lower Mississippi. In those times these states were largely supplied with grain and forage from the Northwestern States. Here you were giving your attention to one or two great staple products, for which you found a large foreign market. I congratulate you that the progress of events has made you not less agricultural, but has diversified your agriculture so that you are not now wholly dependent upon these great staples for the income of your farms. It is a great thing that you are now raising more wheat, more corn, more hogs and cattle; that you are now

raising potatoes and watermelons and cabbage. [Cheers.]
The benefits of this diversification are very great, and
the change symbolizes more than we at first realize.
This change means that we are now coming to understand that meanness cannot be predicted of any honest
industry. I rejoice that you are adding to diversified
agriculture diversified manufacturing pursuits ; that you
are turning your thought to compressing and spinning
cotton as well as raising it. I know no reason why these
cotton states that produce 75 per cent of the cotton of
the world, should not spin the greater portion of it. I
know no reason why they should export it as raw material rather than as a manufactured product, holding in
their midst the profits of this transformation of the raw
material to the finished product. [Applause.] I hope
it may be so. I see evidences that the people are turning
their attention to new industries, and are bringing into
the midst of these farming communities a large population of artisans and laborers, to consume at your own
doors the product of your farms. I am glad that a liberal Government is making this great waterway to the
sea safe and capable of an uninterrupted use. I am glad
that it is here making the shores of your own city con·
venient and safe, and that it is opening, north and south,
an uninterrupted and cheap transportation for the products of all these lands that lie along this great system
of rivers. I am glad that it is bringing you in contact
with ports of the Gulf that look out with near and invit-

ing aspects toward a great trade in South America that we shall soon possess. I am glad to believe that these great river towns will speedily exchange their burdens with American ships at the mouth of the Mississippi, to be transported to foreign ports under the flag of our own country. [Great cheering.]

MAJORITY RULE.

This Government of ours is a compact of the people to be governed by a majority expressing itself by lawful methods. [Cheers.] Everything in this country is to be brought to the measure of the law. I propose no other rule, either as an individual or as a public officer. I can not in any degree lay down this rule [Cries of "No, no," and cheers.] without violating my official duty. There must be no other supremacy than that of lawful majorities. Therefore I think, while I realize and sympathize with your difficulties, we must all come out at last to this conclusion, that the supremacy of the law is the one supremacy in this country of ours. [Cheers.]

Now, my fellow citizens, I thank you for this warm and magnificent demonstration of your respect, accepting cordially the expression of the chief of your city government that you are a sincere, earnest, patriotic, devoted people. I beg to leave with each of you the suggestion that each in his place shall do what he can to maintain social order and public peace; that the laws here and everywhere shall be between the well-disposed

and the ill-disposed. The efforts of speech to this immense throng is too great for me. I beg to assure you
that I carry from the great war of sentiment, no sentiment of ill will to any. [Cheers.] I am glad that
the Confederate soldier, confessing that defeat which
has brought him blessings that would have been impossible otherwise, has been taken again into full participation in the administration of the Government; that no
penalties, limitations or other inflictions rest upon him.
I have taken, and can always take, the hand of a brave
Confederate soldier with confidence and respect. [Great
cheering.] I would put you under one yoke only, and
that is the yoke that the victors in that struggle bore
when they went home and laid off their uniforms—the
yoke of the law and the obligation always to obey it.
[Cheers.] Upon that platform, without distinction between the victors and the vanquished, we enter together
upon possibilities as a people that we cannot overesti-
mate. I believe this nation is lifting itself to a new life;
that this flag shall float on unfamiliar seas, and that this
coming prosperity will be equally shared by all our people. [Prolonged cheering.]

LITTLE ROCK, ARKANSAS.

APRIL 17.

The President and party received a cordial welcome at the State House, where a formal address was made by Governor Eagle.

The President, responding, said:

Gov. Eagle and Fellow Citizens:—No voice is large enough to compass this immense throng. But my heart is large enough to receive all the gladness and joy of your great welcome here to-day. [Applause.] I thank you one and all for your presence, for the kind words of greeting which have been spoken by your Governor, and for these kind faces turned to me. In all this I see a great fraternity; in all this I feel new impulses to a better discharge of every public and every private duty. I cannot but feel that in consequence of this brief contact with you to-day, I shall carry away a better knowledge of your State, its resources, its capabilities, and of the generous warm-heartedness of its people. We have a country whose greatness this meeting evidences, for there are here assembled masses of independent men. The commonwealth rests upon the free suffrage of its citizens, and their devotion to the constitution and flag is the bulwark of its life. [Cheers.] We have agreed, I am sure, that we will do no more fighting among ourselves. [Cries of "Good! good!" and cheers.] I may say to you confidentially that Senator Jones and I agreed

several years ago, after observing together the rifle practice at Fort Snelling, that shooting had been reduced to
such accuracy that war was too dangerous for either of
us to engage in it. [Laughter and cheers.] But, my
friends, I cannot prolong this talk. Once already to-day
in the dampness of this atmosphere I have attempted to
speak, and therefore you will allow me to conclude by
wishing your state, for its Governor and all its public
officers, for all its citizens without exception, high or
humble, the blessing of social order, peace and prosperity, the fruits of intelligence and piety. [Great cheering.]

PALESTINE, TEXAS.

APRIL 18.

Governor Hogg delivered a short address of
welcome :

*Mr. President, Ladies and Gentlemen of the President-
ial Party:*—Texas welcomes you and is proud to have
your visit. In the abundance of their generosity the
people all along your route through the state will give
you a friendly and enthusiastic greeting. Remembering
what you said the other day in Tennessee, we are profoundly impressed with your visit. In the depths of my
heart I am proud that you have come South and to Texas, and again, in behalf of a generous people, I welcome

you to every city, town and hamlet in the State, and we guarantee to you and yours a just, honored and enthusiastic welcome and the best the land affords.

He then introduced the President, who spoke as follows:

Governor Hogg and Fellow Citizens:—It gives me pleasure to come, this fresh morning, into this state—a kingdom without a king and an empire without an emperor, a state gigantic in proportions, matchless in resources, with diversified industries and infinite capacities to sustain a tremendous population, and to bring to every home where industry abides prosperity and comfort. Such homes, I am sure, are represented here this morning—American homes, where the father abides in respect and mother in deep love of children that sit about firesides where all that makes for good is taught and the first rudiments of obedience to law and order in relation one to another are put into the young mind. Out of this comes social order; on this rests the security of our country. The home is the training school for American citizenship. There we learn to defer to others; selfishness is suppressed by the needs of those about us. There self-sacrifice and love, willingness to give ourselves for others, are born. I thank you that so many of you have come here this morning from such homes, and all of us are thankful together that peace rests upon our whole country. All of us have pledged ourselves that no sec-

tional strife shall ever divide us, and that, while abiding
in peace with all the world, we are against all aggression,
one mighty, united people. [Cheers.] I desire to assure
my countrymen that in my heart I make no distinction
between states; no distinction between our people anywhere. [Cheers.] I have a deep desire that everywhere
in all our states there shall be but profound respect for
the will of the majority, expressed by our methods, that
shall bring constant peace into all our communities. It
is very kind of you to come here this morning before
breakfast—perhaps you are initiating me into the Texas
habit; is it so?—of taking something before breakfast.
[Laughter and cheers.] This exhilerating draught of
good will you have given me this morning will not, I
hope, disturb either my digestion or comfort during this
good day. [Cheers.]

HOUSTON, TEXAS.

APRIL 18.

Houston gave the President an enthusiastic
reception. Representative Stewart presented
the president from the balcony of the Capital
Hotel, and in response he spoke as follows:

My Fellow Citizens:—Your faces all respond to the
words of welcome which have been spoken in your be-

half. We have been not only pleased, but touched by the delicate and kindly expressions of regard which we have received since entering the state of Texas. I remained up last night until after midnight that I might not unconsciously pass into this great state, and I was called very early from my bed this morning to receive a draught of welcome before I had breakfasted, from another Texas audience. You have a state whose greatness I think you have discovered. A stranger can hardly hope to point out to you that which you have not already known. Perhaps Virginia and Kentucky have been heard to say more about their respective states than Texas, but I think their voices are likely soon to be drowned by the enthusiastic and affectionate claims which you will present to the country for your great commonwealth. [Cheers.] You have the resources in some measure—in a great measure—of all the states gathered within your borders; a soil adapted to the production of all the cereals and grasses, and to this you add cotton, sugar and tobacco. You are very wisely diversifying your crops, because the history of intelligent farming shows that as the crops are diversified the people prosper. All is not staked upon the success of a single crop. You do well, therefore, to raise cotton, sugar and tobacco, and I am glad you are not neglecting cattle, sheep, hogs, corn and all the cereals. We have been trying to do what we could from Washington to make you a larger and better market for your enormous meat products. [Cheers.] We have felt that the restrictions imposed by some of the European Governments could not fairly be justified upon the ground stated by them. Already the Secretary of Agriculture—himself a farmer who has with his own hands wrought in all the work of the farm—has succeeded in procuring the removal of some of these injurious restrictions, and has announced to the country that the exportation of cattle has increased 100 per cent in the last year. [Cheers.]

I beg to assure you that these interests will have the most careful attention from the Government at Washington and from our representatives at foreign ports. It is believed that we have now, by legislation, a system of sanitary inspection of our meat products that, when once put in operation and examined by the European Government, will remove the last excuse for the exclusion of our meats from these foreign states. Our time is so limited that I can scarcely say more than "thank you." We cannot at all repay you for this demonstration and welcome, but let me say that in all your prosperity I shall rejoice. I do desire that all our legislation and all our institutions and the combined energies of all our people shall work together for the common good of all our states and of all our population. [Great cheering.] You have great resources of a material sort, and yet above all this I rejoice that the timely forethought of your public men has provided an unexampled school fund for the education of the children. These things that partake of the life, that are spiritual, are better after all than the material. Indeed there can be no true prosperity in any state or community where they are not faithfully fostered. Good social order, respect for the law, regard for other men's rights, orderly, peaceful administration, are the essential things in any community.

GALVESTON, TEXAS.

APRIL 19.

At the Beach Hotel, President Harrison responded to the address of welcome by Gen. Wane.

The storm of applause that burst when the President concluded was tremendous. It was the evidence of an enthusiasm that proved that Galvestonians appreciated the distinguished honor of entertaining the head of the General Government, and the kindly treatment of their city at his hands.

The following is the President's speech:

My Fellow Citizens :—We close to-night a whole week of travel, a whole week of hand-shaking, a whole week of talking. I have before me ten thousand miles of hand-shaking and speaking, and I am not, by reason of what this week has brought me, in voice to contend with the

fine but rather strong Gulf breeze which pours in upon
us to-night, and yet it comes to me laden with the fra-
grance of your welcome. [Cheers.] It comes with the
softness, refreshment and grace which has accompanied
all my intercourse with the people of Texas. [Great
cheering.] The magnificent and cordial demonstration
which you have made in our honor to-day will always
remain a bright and pleasant picture in my memory.
[Great cheers.] I am glad to have been able to rest my
eyes upon the city of Galveston. I am glad to have been
able to traverse this harbor, and to look upon that liberal
work which a liberal and united Government has inau-
gurated for your benefit and for the benefit of the North-
West. [Great and prolonged cheers.] I have always
believed that it was one of the undisputed functions of
the general Government to make these great water-ways
which penetrate our country, and these harbors into
which our shipping must come to receive the tribute of
rail and river, safe, commodious and easy of access. This
ministering care should extend to our whole country,
and I am glad that, adopting a policy with reference to
the harbor work here at least, which I insisted upon in a
public message [great and prolonged cheering] the appropriation has been made adequate to a diligent and
prompt completion of the work. [Great cheering.] In
the past the Government has undertaken too many things
at once, and its annual appropriations have been so inadequate that the work of the engineers was much retarded,

and often seriously damaged, in the interval of waiting for fresh appropriations.

It is a better policy, when a work has once been determined to be of national significance, that the appropriation should be sufficient to bring it speedily, and without loss, to a conclusion. [Great cheering.] I am glad that the scheme of the engineer for giving deep water to Galveston is thus to be prosecuted. I have said that some of our South Atlantic and Gulf ports occupy a most favorable position for the new commerce toward which we are reaching out our hands, and which is reaching out its hands to us. [Great cheering.] I am an economist in the sense that I would not waste one dollar of public money, but I am not an economist in the sense that I would leave incomplete or suffer to lag any great work highly promotive of the true interests of our people. [Great cheering.]

RECIPROCITY.

We are great enough and rich enough to reach forward to grander conceptions than have entered the minds of some of our statesmen in the past. If you are content, I am not, that the nations of Europe should absorb nearly the entire commerce of these near sister republics that lie south of us. It is naturally in large measure ours —ours by neighborhood, ours by nearness of access, ours by that sympathy that binds a hemisphere without a king. [Great cheers.] The inauguration of the Pan-American Congress, or more properly the American Conference, the happy conduct of that meeting, the wise and comprehensive measures which were suggested by it, with the fraternal and kindly spirit that was manifested by our southern neighbors, has stimulated a desire in them and in our people for a larger intercourse of commerce and of friendship. The provisions of the bill passed at the last session looking to a reciprocity of trade not only met with my official approval when I signed the bill, but with my zealous promotion before the bill was reported. [Great and prolonged cheers.] Its provision concerning reciprocity is that we have placed upon our free list sugar, tea, coffee and hides, and have said to those nations from whom we receive these great staples: "Give us free access to your ports for an equivalent amount of our produce in exchange, or we will reïmpose duties upon the articles named." The law leaves it wholly with the Executive to negotiate these arrangements. It does not need that they shall take the form of a treaty. They need not be submitted for the concurrence of the Senate. It only needs that we, having made our offer, shall receive their offer in return; and when they have made up an acceptable schedule of articles produced by us that shall have free access to their ports a proclamation by the President closes the whole business. [Cheers.] Already one treaty with that youngest of the South-American republics, the Great Republic of Brazil, has been negotiated and proclaimed I think, without disclosing any executive secret, I may tell you that the arrangement with Brazil is not likely to abide in lonesomeness much longer. [Great and prolonged cheering.] That others are to follow. And that as a result of these trade arrangements, the products of the United States, our meats, our breadstuffs and certain lines of manufactured goods are to find free or favored access to the ports of many of the South and Central American States. All the States will share in these benefits. We have had some analyses made of the manifests of some of our steamers now sailing to South American ports, and in a single steamer it was found that twenty-five of our States contributed to the cargo. But we shall need something more. We shall need American steamships to carry American goods to these ports. [Great cheering.] The last Congress passed a bill appropriating about $1,500,000, and authorized the Postmaster General to contract with steamship companies for a period not exceeding ten years, for the carrying of the United States mail. The foreign mail service is the only mail service out of which the Government has been making a net profit. We do not make a profit out of our land service. There is an annual deficiency, which my good friend, the Postmaster General has been trying very hard to reduce or wipe out. The theory of our mail service is that it is for the people, that we are not to make a profit out of it; that we are to give them as cheap postage as is possible.

CHEAPER POSTAGE.

We are, many of us, looking forward to the time when we shall have one-cent postage in this country. [Cheers.] We have been so close and penurious in dealing with our ships in the carrying of foreign mails that we have actually made revenues out of that business, not having spent for it what we have received from it. Now, we propose to change that policy, and to make more liberal contracts with American lines carrying American mail. [Cheers.] Some one may say we ought not to go into this business—that it is subsidy. But, my friends, every other great nation in the world has been doing it, and is doing it to-day. Great Britain and France have built up their great steamship lines by government aid, and it seems to me our attitude with reference to that is amply protected by an illustration I mentioned the other day. In the olden time no wholesale merchant sent out traveling men to solicit custom, but he stood in his own store and waited for his customers. But presently some enterprising merchant began to send out men with their sample cases to seek the trade, to save the country buyer the cost of the trip to New York or Philadelphia, until finally that practice has became universal; and these active, intelligent traveling men are scurrying this country over, pushing and soliciting in their several lines of business. Now, imagine some conservative merchant in New York saying to himself: "All this is wrong; the trade ought to come to me." If he should refuse to adopt these modern

methods, what would be the result? He must adopt the
new method or go out of business. We have been refus-
ing to adopt the universal method used by our competi-
tors in commerce to stimulate their shipping interests,
and we have gone out of the business. [Laughter and
cheers.] Encouraged by what your spokesman has said
to-night, I venture to declare that I am in favor of going
into business again, and, when it is reëstablished, I hope
Galveston will be in the partnership. [Great cheers.]

It has been the careful study of the Postmaster General in preparing to execute the law to which I have
referred, to see how much increase in routes and ships
we could secure by it. We have said to the few existing
American lines: "You must not treat this appropriation
as a plate of soup to be divided and consumed by your
spirit; you must give us new lines, new ships, increased
trips and new ports of call." Already the steamship lines
are looking over the routes to see what they can do with
a view of increasing their tonnage and in establishing
new lines. The Postmaster General has invited the
attention and suggestion of all the boards of trade of our
seaboard cities. Undoubtedly you have received such a
letter. This appropriation is for one year. What the
future is to be must depend upon the deliberate judgment of the people. If during my term of office they
shall strike down a law that I believe to be beneficent, or
destroy its energy by withholding appropriations, I shall
bow to their will; but I shall feel great disappointment

if we do not make this an era for the revival of American commerce.

AN AMERICAN NAVY.

I so much want that the time shall come when our
citizens, living in temporary exile in foreign ports, shall
now and then see steaming into these distant ports a fine
modern man-of-war, flying the United States flag [cheers [
with the best modern guns on her deck and a brave
American crew in her forecastle. [Cheers.] I want, also,
that in these ports, so long unfamiliar with the American flag, there shall again be found our steamships and
our sailing vessels flying the flag that we all love, and
carrying from our shores the products that these men of
toil have brought to them, to exchange for the products
of other climes.   I think we should add to all this ; happily, it is likely to be accomplished by individual effort
in the early completion of the Nicaragua canal. [Cheers.]
The Pacific coast should no longer be found by sea only
by passage of the Horn.   The short route should be
opened, and it will be ; and then, with this wondrous
stirring among the people of all our States, this awaking
to new business plans and more careful and economical
work, there will come great prosperity to all our people.
Texas will spin more of the cotton that she raises.   The
great States of the South will be discontented with the
old condition that made them simply agricultural States,
and will rouse themselves to compete with the older man-

ufacturing States of the North and East. [Cheers.] The vision I have—all the thoughts I have of this matter—embrace all the States and all my countrymen. I do not think of it as a question of party, I think of it as a great American question. [Cheers.]

By the invitation of the address which was made to me, I have freely spoken my mind to you upon those topics. I hope I have done so without offense or impropriety. [Cries of "No, no," and great cheers.] I could not, on an occasion so full of general good feeling as this, obtrude anything that should induce division or dissent. For all who do dissent I have the most respectful tolerance. The views I hold are the result of some thought and investigation, and as they are of public concern, I confidently submit them to the arbitrament of a brave and enlightened American suffrage. • [Applause and cheers.]

SAN ANTONIO, TEXAS.

APRIL, 20.

In this quaint old city, in the midst of a driving rainstorm, the President received an ovation at the opera house. Mayor Callaghan welcomed him to the city, and in response the President said:

Mr. Mayor and Fellow Citizens :—I very much regret
that frequent speaking in the open air during the past
week and the very heavy atmosphere which we have this
morning has somewhat impaired my voice. I am sure
you will crown your hospitality and kindness by allow-
ing me to speak to you only briefly. I sympathize with
you in the distress which you feel that the day is so un-
propitious for any state demonstration, but I have been
told by one wise in such matters that the rain is worth
$5,000,000 to Western Texas. That being the case, it
greatly moderates our regret. There has come to be a
popular habit of attributing to the President whatever
weather may happen on any demonstration in which he
takes a part. I suppose I may claim credit this morning
for this beneficent rain. [Laughter and applause.] I
generously assure you that, if it is worth as much money
as my friend has estimated, I shall not take more than
half that sum. [Laughter.]

In visiting for a little while this historic city, I had
anticipated great pleasure in looking upon the remains of
an earlier occupancy of this territory in which you now
dwell. Our glances this morning must be brief and im-
perfect ; but the history has been written, and the traditions of the martyrdom which occurred here for liberty
are fresh in your minds and are still an inspiring story
to be repeated to your children. I remember in my early
boyhood to have heard in our family thrilling descriptions
of the experiences of an uncle whose name I bear, in some

of these campaigns for freedom in Texas, in which he took a part, so that the story, to me, goes back to these dim early recollections of childhood. I am glad to stand where these recollections are revived and freshened, for they are events of momentous importance to this country, to this state, and to the whole Union. I rejoice that you have here so great a commonwealth.

The stipulations under which Texas came into the Union of states, and which provided that the great commonwealth might be subdivided into five states, seems not to attract much attention in Texas now. Indeed, so far as I can judge, no man would be able successfully to appeal to the suffrage of any hamlet in Texas upon the issue that the state should be divided at all. [Cheers.] The great industrial capabilities, the beneficent climate that spreads over much of your vast territory, the great variety of productions which your soil and climate render possible for the future prominence of the great state of the Union, seems to me can scarcely fail to bring Texas to the front among our great sisterhood. [Cheers.] You are only now beginning to bring to the plow this vast stretch of fertile land; you are only now beginning to diversify those interests, to emancipate yourselves by producing at home in your own fields all of these products which are necessary to comfortable existence. I hope you are soon to add—indeed, you are now largely adding—to this diversity of agricultural pursuits a diversity of mechanical pursuits. The advantages which you have to transmute

the great product of the field into the manufactured product is very great. There can certainly be no reason
why a very large part of the million bales of cotton which
you produce should not be spun in Texas. [Cheers.] I
hope your people will more and more turn their thoughts
to this matter for, just in proportion as a community or
state suitably divides its energies among various interests,
so does she retain the wealth in products and increase
its population. [Applause.]

A great Englishman visiting this country some time
ago, in speaking of the impressions which were made
upon his mind, said he was constantly asked as he traveled through the country whether he was not amazed at
its territorial extent. He said while this, of course, was
a noticable incident of travel, he wondered that he did
not forget all our bigness of territory in a contemplation
of the great spectacle we presented as a free people of organized and peaceful communities. He regarded this
side of our country and her institutions as much more
imperative than its material development or its territorial extent, and he was right in that judgment. My fellow citizens, the pride of America, that which should attract the admiration and has attracted the imitation of
many people upon the face of the earth, is our system of
government. [Applause.] I am glad to know, and have
expressed my satisfaction before, that here in the state
of Texas you are giving attention to education ; that you
have been able to erect a school fund, the interest upon

which promises a most magnificent endowment for your common schools. These schools are the pride and safety of the state. They gather into them upon a common level the children of the rich and poor. In the state in which I dwell, everybody's children attend the common schools. This lesson of equality, the perfect system which has been developed by the method of instruction, is training a valuable class of citizens to take up the responsibilities of government when we shall lay them down. [Applause.] I hope every one of your communities, even your scattered rural communities, will pursue this good work. I am sure this hope is shared by my honored friend, Governor Hogg, who sits behind me, [Applause.] and who in the discharge of his public duties can influence the progress of this great measure.

No material greatness, no wealth, no accumulation of splendor are to be compared with these humble and home-ly virtues which have generally characterized our American homes. The safety of the state, the good order of the community the capacity indeed to produce ma-terial wealth, is dependent upon intelligence and so-cial order. [Applause.] Wealth and commerce are timid creatures. They must be assured that the rest will be safe before they build. So it is always in these communities where the most perfect order is maintained; where intelligence is protected; where the church of God and the institutions of religion are revered and re-

spected, that we find the largest development in material
wealth. [Applause.]

Thanking you for your cordial greeting, all of your
people, and especially the Governor of your state, for
courtesies which have been unfailing, for a cordiality and
friendliness that have not found any stint or repression
in the fact that we are of different political opinions,
[Great cheering] I beg to thank you for this special
manifestation of respect and to ask you to excuse me from
further speech. I shall follow such arrangements as your
committee have made, and shall be glad if in those arrangements there is some provision by which I may
meet as many of you as possible individually. [Pro-
longed cheers.]

EL PASO, TEXAS.

APRIL 21.

The reception at El Paso was a remarkable
event in the history of that city, as a governor
of a foreign state and a general of a foreign
army come many miles to represent their government and join with the citizens of El Paso to
do honor to the President of the United States.
The reception was held at the Court House and
the entire lawn was filled with a crowd of thou-

sands of people, and the balconies and roof of the court house were crowded with many more. On the platform, besides the presidential party, were the envoys of the Republic of Mexico, the civil and state authorities attired in full dress, and the military in full uniform with their magnificent decorations.

Addresses were made as follows:

Col. Villaneve, representing President Diaz of Mexico —Mr. President, in the name of the Mexican government and secretary of war, I have the honor to extend to you a cordial welcome, accompanied by an earnest desire for your personal prosperity as well as the people you represent. I further congratulate you in the name of my government upon this, your visit to the frontier, more particularly as you are the first President visiting the border.

Gov. Lauro Carillo, Governor of Chihauhau—Mr. President, in the name of the government of the state of Chihauhau, which I represent, also in the name of the authorities and citizens of Juarez, Mexico, I have the honor to extend to you a cordial welcome accompanied with our highest esteem for you.

Gen. Rangel, Department Commander of the Mexican troops—Mr. President, we are here to greet you in the

name of the military and greet you as the standard
bearer of the nation of prosperity.

All the speeches by the Mexican officers were
in the Mexican tongue, and were translated to
the President by an interpreter.

President Harrison delivered what is con-
ceded to be a masterly effort.

The following is the President's speech:

My Fellow Citizens:—We have been journeying for
several days through the great state of Texas. We are
now about to leave this state and receive from you this
parting salutation. Our entrance into this state was with
every demonstration of respect and enthusiasm. This
greeting by the citizens of El Paso and Mexico is a fitting close. I am glad to stand at this gateway of trade
with the great Republic of Mexico. [Applause.] I am
glad to know it is also the gateway of friendship. [Ap-
plause.] I receive with unbounded satisfaction these
tributes of respect that have been brought to me by the
government of Chihauhau and the Mexican military.
[Great applause.]

I desire to extend to all our visitors, not only my personal regard, but the continued assurance of respect of the
American people. [Applause.] I look forward to a
large development of trade. We have passed that era in
our history when we were unpleasant neighbors. We

have come to a time when we cease to covet their possessions, but only covet their friendship, [Great applause] and now to you I bring congratulations for the development you are making. [Applause.] I extend the most cordial congratulations for future prosperity. [Great applause.] I rejoice that these influences that tend to soften the asperities of life, viz., the home, the school and the church, have kept pace with the enterprise and progress, and are to be found among you. [Applause.]

You cannot attract foreign capital or increase citizenship unless you have a reputation for social order. I trust that as your city grows you will see that these foundations are carefully laid, and you may hope that a magnificent superstructure shall rise in its stead

To my comrades of the G. A. R. I wish to extend my most heart-felt greetings, who were magnanimous to the vanquished as well as to the victor, and who only laid upon the vanquished the yoke of obedience to the law. [Loud applause.]

You will excuse me further speech. Again, sirs (to the Mexican visitors), I thank you for this kind greeting. And to you, my countrymen, I extend my heart-felt thanks, and wish you good-bye.

NEW MEXICO'S WELCOME.

While the Presidential train was speeding over the plains of New Mexico, Gov. Prince made the following address of welcome to the President :

As we crossed the Rio Grande we entered the con-fines of New Mexico, and I wish, on behalf of all our people, to express our high gratification at your visit, and to extend our heartiest welcome to the Territory. We welcome you not only as the Chief Magistrate of the Nation, but especially as the President who has shown the greatest interest in our welfare, and who has done the most to promote it.

*   *   *   *   *   *

For forty years New Mexico has suffered from the uncertainty of these titles, and that message, supple-mented by the special message of last July, and by the active interest of members of the cabinet, has brought to us the greatest boon in our history, and opened a future of vast prosperity. Our people feel the deepest gratitude for this recognition and timely aid, and our official wel-come is made personally more heartfelt on this account.

The President returned his thanks in a brief speech.

INDIO, CALIFORNIA.

APRIL, 22.

When the President's party reached Indio it was received by a large and influential delegation, including Gov. Markham and staff, ex-Gov. Perkins, Senator Felton, Judge Van Vleet of Sacramento, S. M. White of Los Angeles, C. F. Crocker, Vice President of the Southern Pacific Railroad, and Mr. Stump, chairman of the Republican committee. Gov. Markham made an address of welcome on behalf of all the the people of the State.

The President responded as follows:

I would not undertake while almost choked with the dust of the plains we have just left, to say all that I hoped to say in the way of pleasant greetings to the citizens of California. Some time when I have been refreshed by your olive oil and your vineyards I would endeavor to express my gratification at being able to visit California. I have long desired to visit your state, and it was the objective point of this trip. I have seen the Northern Coast, Puget Sound, but have never before been able to see California. I remember from boyhood the excitement of the discovery of gold, and have always distantly followed California's growth and progress. Its acquisition was second only to that of Louisiana and the control of the Mississippi river. It strengthened this great coast and made impossible the ownership of a foreign power on any of our coast line. It has held perfect our magnificent insolation, which is our great pro-

tection against foreign aggression. I thank you, gentlemen for your kindly reception, and assure you that if I
should have complaint to make of my treatment in California it would be because its people have been too hospitable.

COLTON, CALIFORNIA.
APRIL 22.

The President was welcomed by an enthusiastic crowd, nearly all of whom pressed up to
the platform of the train and shook hands with
him. Flags helped to swell the throng. He was
introduced by Gov. Markham and made a short
patriotic address.

The following is the President's address :

My Fellow Citizens:—We have traveled now something more than 3,500 miles. They have been 3,500 miles
of cordial greeting from my fellow citizens; they have
been 3,500 miles of perpetual talk. It would require a
brain more fertile in its resources, more diversified in its
operations than the state of California in its productions,
to say something original or interesting at each one of
the stopping places, but I can say always with a warm
heart to my fellow citizens who greet me so cordially,
who look to me out of such kindly faces—I thank you.
I am your servant in all things that will conduce to the

general prosperity and happiness of the American people. Remote from us far east in distance, we are united to you not only by ties of common citizenship, by the reverence and honor we joyfully give to one flag, but by the changes of emigration which have brought so many of the people of the older states to you. At every station which I have stopped since entering California some Hoosier has reached up his hand to greet me, [Laughter and cheers] and the omnipresent Ohio man of course I have found everywhere. I was assured by these gentlemen that they were making their full contributions to the development of your country, and that they had possessed themselves of their fair share of it. I have been greatly pleased this morning to come out of the land of the desert and drifting sand into this land of homes and smiling women and bright children. I have been glad to see these beautiful gardens, these fertile fields, and to know that your economical collection and distribution of the waters of the hills made all these valleys to smile like a garden of Eden. We do not come as spies to look at your land with any view of dispossessing you, as the original spies went into Palestine. We come simply to exchange friendly greetings, and we shall hope to carry away nothing that does not belong to us. [Cheers.] If we shall leave your happy and prosperous state freighted with your good will and love, as we shall leave ours with you, it will be a happy exchange. [Cheers.]

POMONA, CALIFORNIA.
APRIL, 22.

The Presidential party reached here at 1 o'clock and stopped twenty minutes. Only two hours' notice of the stop had been given, but the whole town turned out. H. Z. Osborne introduced the President, who spoke as follows:

You will surely excuse me from extended remarks. I have been subjected to such a strain that my brain needs irrigation to put it in trim again. [Cheers.] I am glad to look at faces of American citizens. No such people gather in any other country as greet me at every station. They come from good homes, the safety of the commonwealth. I am pleased to see these children. Schools have everywhere followed the western Pioneers. You have New England education and homes. More than that; you have the New England idea of thrift, living on little and having much over.

LOS ANGELES, CALIFORNIA.
APRIL, 22.

In point of weather, attendance and enthusiasm and reception given by the people of Los Angeles to President Harrison was all that could be desired.

The demonstration both in front of the City Hall after the parade and in the evening at the Pavilion was imposing. The interior of the Pavilion had been beautifully decorated, but the effect of the floral devices was almost swallowed up in the sea of humanity which had poured into the building.

A platform had been erected on the City Hall steps, and when the procession came to a halt at that point, Mayor Hazard made a short address followed by Gov. Markham, who spoke briefly, introducing the President.

The following are the president's remarks:

My Fellow Citizens:—My stay among you has been not only long enough to form an individual judgment of the quality of your people, but it has been long enough to get a large idea of the number of them. [Laughter.] I beg you to accept my most sincere and grateful thanks for this magnificent demonstration of your respect. I do not at all assume that these hurrahs and flowers and streaming banneis with which you have greeted me to-day are at all a tribute to me individually. I receive them as a most magnificent welcome, assuring demon- stration of the love of the people of California for Amer- ican institutions. [Applause.] And well are these institutions worthy of all honor The flag that you have

displayed today, the one flag, the banner of the free, and
the symbol of an inseparable union, [cheers] is worthy
of the affections of our people. Men have died for it on
the field of battle; women have consecrated it with their
tears and prayers, as they placed the standard in the hands
of brave men going to battle.   It is historically full of tender interests and pride.   It was a glorious symbol on the
sea, in those days when the American navy maintained its
prestige and successfully fought the navies of the world.
[Cheers.]

It is a proud record of the land, from the time of our
great struggle for independence, down to the last sad
conflict between ourselves. We bless God today, and
those brave men, who, working out his purposes on the
field of battle, made it again the symbol of a united people. [Applause.]   Our institutions, of which this flag
is the type and emblem, are free institutions.   These men
and women, into whose faces I look, are free men and
free women.   I do not honor you by my presence today,
I hold my trust from you, and you honor me. [Cheers.]

This magnificent domain of the Pacific Coast, seized
for the Union by the energy and courage and wise forethought of Fremont and his associates, is essential to our
perfection of territory.   Nothing more important—unless
it be the possession of the Territory of Louisiana and
the control of the Mississippi River--has ever occurred
in our national history. [Applause] We touch from
ocean to ocean, and on both we are building magnificent

commonwealths, and are thus securing that historical individuality and isolation, which comes as assurance of perpetual peace. [Cheers.]

No great conflict of arms will again ever take place on American territory if we are true to ourselves, and I have therefore determined that no civil conflict shall again rend our country. [Applause.] We are a peace-loving nation, and yet we cannot be sure that everybody else will be peaceful. [Cheers and laughter.] And, therefore, I am glad that by the general consent of our people, by liberal appropriations from Congress, we are putting on the sea some of the best vessels of their class afloat [Applause.]

And we are now prepared to put upon their decks as good guns as are made in the world. And when we have completed our programme, ship by ship, we will put in their forecastle as brave Jack Tars as serve under any flag. [Great applause.] The provident care of the Government should be given to your seacoast defenses until all these great ports of the Atlantic and Pacific are made safe.

But, my countrymen, this audience overmatches a voice that has been in exercise from remote Virginia to Los Angeles. [Applause.] I bid you, therefore, again to receive my most hearty thanks and congratulations, and to excuse me from further speech

AT THE PAVILION.

People began gathering in front of the pavilion before it was fairly dark. No sooner was the cry passed along through the crowd, "open doors," than the great throng pressed forward and a moving, quivering tide of humanity struggled and surged through the doorways, and 10,-000 men, women and children poured like a human avalanche into the building.

The scene on the main floor was one of the most impressive—as regards a crowd—ever witnessed here. Probably never in the history of Los Angeles has there been such a gathering. Every one of her 50,000 inhabitants were apparently on hand to welcome the chief of the nation by appearing personally on this occasion. The President made a short address as follows:

Fellow Citizens:—I thank you for this demonstration, because I am sure that it is non-partisan in its character and is meant to express the general good will which you bear toward me irrespective of party. This was more particularly illustrated to me to-day at a small station not far from here by a man who insisted on shaking hands with me even if he did lose $1,000 over my election. I am induced to feel from the assurances of respect and esteem which I have received everywhere from the sovereigns of this country, that I shall have no trouble as to the carrying out of their wishes satisfactorily in the future as I have in the past. My countrymen, I thank you sincerely for the splendid reception you have accorded to me and trust you will believe me when I tell you that I am at a loss to find words with which to express my admiration of your beautiful, magnificent and prosperous city of Los Angeles.

SAN DIEGO, CALIFORNIA.

APRIL 23.

The President came, saw the city of the Silver Gate, and won the admiration of every man and woman, and fluttered the hearts of 2,000 flower-laden school children.

Early in the morning the INDIANA ASSOCIATION numbering about one hundred members, met the President in the reception room of the Hotel Coronado. Mrs. George D. Copeland presented Mrs. Harrison with a floral miniature of the state which they all at one time called home. The piece was about two feet square and consisted of a bed of carnations and violets, on which had been raised the name "Indiana" in blue violets.

The formal presentation of the address drawn up by the state's representatives was made by L. A. Wright. The document had been neatly embossed on heavy paper and was intended to be carried away by the president as a souvenir.

He acknowledged the address with a bow and replied as follows :

My Friends:—I regret that I can only say thank you. Our time is now due to the citizens of San Diego and I have promised not to detain that committee. It is particularly pleasurable to me to see, as I have done at almost every station where our train stopped, some Indianian, who stretched up the hand of old neighborship to greet me as I passed along. It is this intermingling of our people which obtains the merit of the home. The Yankee intermingles with the Illinoisian, the Hoosier with the Sucker and the people of the South with them all; and it is this commingling which gives that unity which marks the American nation.

I am glad to know that there are so many of you here, and as I said to some Hoosier as I came along, I hope you have secured your share of these blessings of life

The reception at the Plaza was witnessed by at least four thousand people, after the Presidential party had been driven over the city. All along the line of march the decorations were very handsome, flowers and floral decorations were in lavish profusion. The carriage of the President and Mrs. Harrison was literally filled with flowers. School children to the number of 2,000, liberally provided with calla lillies and roses, were formed along the line of march, and as the President passed by the crowd showered him with flowers and scattered blossoms beneath the feet of his horses, so that he passed along a continuous floral pathway. As the procession passed the army barracks the regulation salute was fired.

Mayor Gunn read an address of welcome, briefly reciting the history of San Deigo, and then presented the President, who spoke as follows :

Mr. Mayor and Fellow Citizens:—I am in slavery to a railroad schedule and have but a few moments longer to tarry in your beautiful city. If there were no other reward for our journey across the continent what we have seen to-day about your magnificent harbor would have repaid us for all the toil of travel. [Applause.] I do not come to tell you anything about California, for I have already perceived in my intercourse with Californians in the east, and during this brief stay among you, that already you know all about California. [Laughter.] You are, indeed, most happily situated. Every element that makes life comfortable is here. Every possibility that makes life successful and prosperous is here; and I am sure, as I look into these kindly, upturned faces, that your homes have as healthful a moral atmosphere as God has spread over your smiling land.

It is with regret that we now part from you. The welcome you have extended to us is magnificent, kindly and tasteful. We shall carry away the most pleasant impression, and shall wish for you all that you anticipate in your largest dreams for your beautiful city—that your harbor may be full of foreign and coast-wise traffic, that it may not be long until the passage of our naval and merchant marine shall not be by the Horn, but by Nicaragua. [Cheers.] I believe that great enterprise, which is to bring your commerce into nearer and cheaper contact with the Atlantic seaboard cities, both of this continent and of South America, will not be long delayed.

And now, again, with the most grateful thanks for your friendly attention in my own behalf and in behalf of all who journey with me, I bid you a most kindly farewell.

INTERNATIONAL COURTESIES.

Mayor Gunn introduced Governor Torres before the president had taken his seat and the latter, addressing Mr. Harrison, said:

I have received a telegram which I have the honor to read to you. The translation is as follows:

It has come to my knowledge that the President of the United States, Hon. Benjamin Harrison, shall visit San Diego on the 23d instant, and I let you know it, so that you may call and congratulate him in my name, and present him with my compliments.

[Signed.] PORFIRIO DIAZ."

In reply to this kindly message the president felt called upon to speak again, and he said:

Governor Torres:—This message from that progressive and intelligent gentleman who presides over the destinies our sister republic is most grateful to me. I assure you that all our people, that the government through all its instituted authorities, entertain for President Diaz and for the chivalrous people over which he presides, the most friendly sentiments of respect. [Cheers and applause.] We covet, sir, your good will and those

mutual exchanges which are mutually profitable, and we
hope that the two republics may forever dwell in fraternal peace.

Governor Torres made answer ; The Mexican people correspond heartly to your kind
wishes.

After a delightful trip from San Diego, over
a route abounding with beautiful scenery,
the pre idential party arrived at Pasadena at
7.40 p. m.   Short stops were made at Oceanside,
Santa Ann, Orange and at Riverside.   The
President received a cordial welcome at each of
these places, and expressed his thanks in brief
speeches complimentary to the people and their
country.

The crowd at each of these places was swelled
by school children, who presented the ladies
of the party with flowers.   The reception took
place in a float pavilion surmounted with a fine
specimen of the American eagle.   The party
left the train at Arlington Station, six miles
from Riverside and drove to the town in flower-be
decked carriages through a continuous lane of

oranges groves and the celebrated Magnolia avenue. On reaching the High school they were received by a large crowd, including hundreds of school children with waving flags. The formal reception took place at Glenwood Hotel where the President was introduced by Gov. Markham and made a short address.

PASADENA, CALIFORNIA.

APRIL, 23.

Immediately after the arrival of the train, about eight o'clock in the evening, the President held a public reception in the office of Hotel Green and later in the evening the banquet was served in the dining room, which was beautifully decorated with flowers ; in fact the entire hotel was fragrant and beautiful with its profusion of flowers, and the chambers of the guests were lavishly filled with great clusters and banks of them. At the banquet Mr. Buchanan proposed the health of President Harrison and briefly referred to the honor and pleasure conferred by the visit of the President.

In response the President said:

Fellow Citizens:—It affords me great pleasure to acknowledge the honor paid me by the people of Pasadena,
and I hope to see your beautiful city by sunlight, when I
will be able to better appreciate its glories, and to have
my impression confirmed of a place I was prepared to
believe the gem of California. [Applause.] No other
town in this state has been more familiarly known to me
by reputation than Pasadena, except San Francisco, a
fact due to the circumstance that Indiana people had
founded it. A number of my neighbors, among them
the gentleman who has just proposed the toast in my
honor, have come here and earned the esteem of the
community they had helped to form. It is pleasant to
renew friendships here. I have found Hoosiers all along
the line of our travel, and Ohio men pop up too, on all
sides, which is not surprising. They are apt to be found
in the vicinity of public office. [Laughter.] What good
fortune has befallen me in political life I trace to the
fact that I am a Buckeye by birth. [Applause.]

California is full of affectionate interest for all of us,
for here we look into the shining eyes and pleasant faces
of a contented and happy people. You occupy a fortunate position and your history has been a succession of
fortunate surprises, the most surprising being the process of converting apparently barren plains into gardens
that are unequaled for productiveness. [Applause.]

And now, when I remind you that it was 12 o'clock last night when we retired and that reveille sounded at 6 this morning, you will permit me to say good night.

APRIL 24.

The President and party were treated to a beautiful floral display this morning during a two-hour drive through the principal streets of this crown of the valley.

At a point on the drive on Marengo avenue the procession passed under a large arch composed principally of California lilies and having a base of rare tropical plants. School children were congregated about this arch, and they showered President and Mrs. Harrison with such a profusion of bouquets that those who followed passed over a veritable bed of flowers. Soon afterward the procession passed through a gate of flowers operated by two little girls.

SANTA BARBARA, CALIFORNIA.

APRIL. 24.

The day was nearly perfect, only enough clouds floating about to soften the effect of the

mountains. From early morning crowded
vehicles arrived from the country districts. The
streets were alive with people the decorations
were elaborate and handsome, the parade was a
novelty in its way, the battle of flowers was a
surprise even to those who expected much of it
and the Spanish dances delighted the visiting
party.

In the block above the Arlington Hotel was
located the President's reviewing stand and opposite it a stand accommodating about 300 people, between which the battle of flowers took
place. The President's stand was a floral
triumph. The front of it was filled in with a
solid bank of bright colored flowers. Some idea
of the extent of the decorations may be formed
when it is known that nearly 20,000 calla lilies
were used on the President's stand alone, one
person (Mr. Sexton, of Goleta) having sent in
9,000 calla blossoms. The stand opposite was
also beautifully trimmed. A most exquisite
feature of the parade was that of the "tubs."
Over a hundred flower-trimmed equipages were
in line, no two being similar in color or design.

A better proof could not have been given of the marvelous flora of Santa Barbara in the month of April. The carts were covered entirely with flowers of every hue.

The last maneuvre before the grand stand was the battle of flowers between both countermarching columns. It began with a deadly flourish of fans, parasols and flags. From the stand down to the arch of welcome the air was at one time bright with flowers. Sprays, wreaths and tied bunches hurled from side to side. Heavy ordinance of made bouquets did splendid work and caused many a gorgeous, mounted cavalier to dodge ingloriously. Over all fell a pyrotechnic shower of single blossoms. The air was a floral rainbow and the pavement a carpet of crushed sweets. The battle was waged with much spirit and not at all confined to the marchers.

Gen. Vandever delivered a short address of welcome on behalf of the people of Santa Barbara, referring especially to the mingling of the American and Spanish races in a loyal love for their common country.

President Harrison responded as follows :

General Vandever, Gentlemen of the Committee and Friends:—If I have been in any doubt as to the fact of the perfect identity of your people with the American nation, that doubt has been dissipated by one incident which has been prominent in all this trip, and that is that the great and predominant and all pervading American habit of demanding a speech on every occasion, has been characteristically prominent in California. [Laughter.] I am more than delighted by this visit to your city. It has been made brilliant with the display of banners and flowers; one the emblem of our national greatness and prowess, the other the adornment which God has to beauty nature. With all this I am sure I have read in the faces of the men, women and children who have greeted me, that these things, these flowers of the field, and this flag representing organized government—typify what is to be found in the homes of California. The expression of your welcome to-day has been unique and tasteful beyond description. I have not the words to express the high sense of appreciation, and the amazement that filled the minds of all our party as we looked upon this display which you improvised for our reception. No element of beauty, no element of taste, no element of gracious kindness has been lacking in it all; and for that we tender you our most hearty thanks. We shall keep this visit as a bright spot in our memories. [Applause.]

After the public reception the President and party were escorted to the dining room of the Arlington which had been transformed into a ball room, where the visitors witnessed the Spanish dance. A space in front of the President's party was kept clear as the slow and graceful Spanish Contra Danza was danced.

A special figure "Salute to the President" which was invented for the occassion, was introduced as the first figure and proved a very beautiful innovation.

SANTA PAULA, CALIFORNIA.

APRIL 24.

At Santa Paula the President was cordially received. Here was displayed the largest solid floral piece the party had seen since it left Washington. It was in the form of a signboard, twelve feet long and three feet wide, and was made entirely of calla lilies. Across its face was the word "Welcome," in large letters of red geraniums. The President addressed the crowd as follows:

My Friends:—I cannot feel myself a stranger in this state so distant from home, when I am greeted by some familiar face from my Indiana at almost every station. Your fellow citizen who has spoken in your behalf was an old time Indianapolis friend. I hope he is held in the same esteem which he was held by the people among whom he spent his early years as a boy and man. [Cries of " he is."] That you should have gone to the pains to make such magnificent decorations and to come out in such large numbers for this momentary greeting very deeply touches my heart.

I have never seen in any state of the Union what seems to me to be a more happy and contented people than I have seen this morning. Your soil and sun are genial, healthful and productive, and I have no doubt that these genial and kindly influences are manifested in the homes that are represented here, and that there is sunshine in the household as well as in the fields; that there is contentment and love and sweetness in these homes as well as in these gardens that are so adorned with flowers. Our pathway has been strewn with flowers we have literally driven for miles over flowers that in the East would have been priceless, and these favors have all been acompanied with manifestations of friendliness for which I am very grateful, and everywhere there has been set up as having greater glory than the sunshine, greater glory than the flowers, this flag of our country. [Applause.]

Everywhere I have been greeted by some of these comrades, veterans of the late war, whose presence among you should be an inspiration to increase patriotism and loyalty. I bid them an affectionate greeting, and am sorry I cannot tarry with them longer. [Cheers.]

BAKERSFIELD, CALIFORNIA.

APRIL 25.

The train remained here only ten minutes, and the welcome was a cordial one. Judge A. R. Conkling presented the President. He was about to respond when he was assailed by such a shower of bouqets that he was forced to seek shelter in his car. Finally he addressed them as follows:

My Friends:—I am very much obliged to you for your friendly greeting and for these bouquets. You must excuse me if I seem a little shy of bouquets. I received one in my eye the other day which gave me a good deal of trouble. You are very kind to meet us here so early in the morning with this cordial demonstration. It has been a very long journey, and has been accompanied with some fatigue of travel, but we feel this morning, in this exhilaration and this sweet sunshine, and refreshed

with your kind greeting, as bright and more happy than
we left the national capital. I am glad to feel that here,
on the western edge of the continent, in this Pacific
State, there is that same enthusiastic love for the flag,
that same veneration and respect for American institutions, for the one Union and the one Constitution, that is
found in the heart of our country. We are one people
absolutely. We follow not men, but institutions. We
are happy in the fact that men may live, die, come or
go, we have still that towards which the heart of the
American citizens turns with confidence and veneration
—this great Union of States devised so happily by our
fathers. Gen. Garfield, when Mr. Lincoln was stricken
down by the foul hand of the assassin, when that great
wave of dismay and grief swept over the land, standing
in a busy thoroughfare of New York, could say, "The
Government at Washington still lives."   It is dependent
upon no man, lodged safely in the affections of the people, and having its impregnable defense and its assured
perpetuity in their love and veneration for law. [Cheers.]

TULARE, CALIFORNIA.

APRIL. 25.

The President and party, which included
Gov. Markham, ex-Gov. Perkins, Mr. Stump
and Col. Crocker, received a regular ovation.

The party was escorted to a gayly decorated stand, the base of which was the stump of a mammoth redwood tree. This was surrounded by a guard of honor composed of the local militia and Grand Army posts. The President was introduced by Gov. Markham, and was greeted with hearty applause. He addressed the assemblage as follows :

My Friends:—This seems to be a very happy and smiling audience, and I am sure that the gladness which is in your hearts and in your faces does not depend at all upon the presence of this little company of strangers who tarry with you for a moment. It is born of influences and conditions that are permanent. It comes of the happy sunshine and sweet air that is over your fields, and still more from the contentment, prosperity and love and peace that are in your households. California has been spoken of as a wonderland, and everywhere we have gone something new, interesting and surprising has been presented to our observation. There has been but one monotone in our journey, and that is the monotone of universal welcome from all your people. [Cheers.]

FRESNO, CALIFORNIA.

APRIL 25.

The reception was short, the train stopping
only ten minutes, but it was enthusiastic and
one to be remembered by the people of Fresno,
as well as by the entire party to whom it was
tendered. Mayor Cole, Dr. Chester Rowell and
Hon. W. W. Morrow were introduced to the
party. Dr. Rowell stepped to the front of the
platform, made a short but patriotic speech and
introduced the President.

Mr. Fellow Citizens:—It is altogether impossible for
me to reach, with my voice this vast concourse of friends.
I receive with great satisfaction and profound feelings of
gratification this momento which you have given me of
the varied products of this most fertile and happy valley,
I shall carry it with me to Washington as a reminder of
a scene that will never fade from my memory. [Applause.]

It is very pleasant to know that while all these pursuits are carried on, while so much is doing to engage
your thoughts and to industriously employ your time,
they have not in the least turned your minds away from
the love of the flag and of those institutions which spread
their secure power over all your homes. You are in a
free land. No policeman is at your door. Our party

passes through this land without a guard at the car window. You and I are in the safe keeping of a free country's laws. [Cheers.] I am glad to receive from you
this manifestation of your respect. I am glad to drink
in this morning with this sunshine and this sweet balmy
air, a new impulse to public duty, and a new love for the
Union and the flag. [Cheers.] You must excuse me
from further speaking. It is a matter of great regret
that the limits of the time which is given to this journey
as well as its great extent put heavy limitation on the
extent of a single delay. More strongly than any of you,
I wish that it were possible to remain with you longer.

MERCED, CALIFORNIA.

APRIL 25.

The President made the following address
to a large crowd here:

My Fellow Citizens:—I have scarcely been able to fin-
ish a meal since I have been in California. [Laughter.]
I hardly find myself seated at the table till some one
reminds me that in about five minutes I am to meet
another throng of cordial and friendly people, but I think
I could have subsisted on this trip through California
without anything to eat, and have dined all the while
upon the stimulus and inspiration which your good will
and kindly greetings have given me. I do not think,

however, from what I have seen of these valleys that it will be necessary for anyone but the President to live without eating. [Laughter.] I have been greatly delighted with the agricultural richness, with surprises in natural scenery and in the productions which have met us on this journey. But let me say above all these fruits and flowers, above all their productions of the mine and field, I have been most pleased with the men and women of California. [Applause.] It gives me great pleasure we meet everywhere these little ones. I am fond of children ; they attract my interest always and the little ones of my own household furnish about the only relaxation and pleasure I have at Washington. [Applause.]

SAN FRANCISCO, CALIFORNIA.

APRIL 25.

President Harrison was welcomed by a great display of enthusiasm. The presidential train arrived at Oakland about 7 o'clock, and the party were met by a reception committee of citizens. Gen. Ruger and staff, of the regular army, and Gen. Diamond and staff of the State troops escorted them to the large steamer Piedmont. She did not cross to San Francisco at once, but steamed around the bay slowly to enable the President to witness the brilliant illuminations on the bay and on the hills in the city. As the steamer left the wharf at Oakland a signal rocket was sent up from the bow, and instantly bonfires blazed from a dozen elevated points in San Francisco. The Piedmont passed between two long lines of vessels from Oakland to San Francisco, including the United States cruiser Charleston, several revenue cutters and coast survey steamers and a number of ocean-going steamers of the Australia, China and other lines. All of these vessels, as well as every craft lying at the docks on both sides of the bay, were brilliantly illuminated by red fire and electric lights which displayed their decorations of flags and bunting.

APRIL 27.

Van Ness avenue is famed for its great breadth, but it was all to narrow too accommodate the thousands of school children, their teachers and all that great surging crowd of humanity that wanted to see the President.

The enthusiasm of the children knew no bounds. The President bowed as often as he could, for he was kept busy taking the nosegays from the hands of the venturesome children, who ran close up to the wheels to hand the President their flowers. Soon the carriage was a perfect bed of flowers. Still the children came and the great man reached out and took them all and smiled and said "Thank you" as fast as he could.

When the carriage at last reached Golden Gate avenue the speed was quickened, and soon the Presidential party had left the great crowd behind.

PARK AND OCEAN.

Golden Gate Park never looked more like an earthly paradise than it did when the President drove up the wide avenue to the conservatory, and when, on the road to the Cliff House, the Pacific ocean burst upon his view, never was the white foam of the breakers whiter, the blue and opal and green of the restless waters more vivid or the voices of the mighty deep blended in a grander chorus of welcome on the way from the park. Mr. Adolph Sutro met the party and extended an invitation to visit Sutro Heights and take luncheon, which was accepted.

In the evening the President attended a banquet given in his honor by California Alpha Chapter of the State University of Phi Delta Theta fraternity. Mr. Harrison is a member of Ohio Alpha of Miami University of this fraternity of the class of 1852.

Mr. N. E. Wilson introduced the guest of the evening in a few well-chosen remarks and proposed the health of "the President." Mr. Harrison responding, said:

My Friends and Brothers in this old society:—I enjoy this moment very much in being able to associate with you. I was a member of the first chapter of this fraternity, which you all know was founded at Miami University, Oxford, O. I have not lost the impression of solemnity and reverence which I experienced hunting in the dark in those early times to find my chapter room, and I am very glad to know that those meetings were not meetings in the dark. I belonged to the order when it was young, and now I find its members scattered in all States where they all hold positions of trust and influence. I find that in its history it has produced nothing discreditable to itself, but always something of which we may all well be proud. I thank you for these few moments of association with you.

SAN JOSE, CALIFORNIA.
APRIL. 29.

From a beautiful stand, canopied with roses, on the grounds of the Hotel Rudome, Mayor Rucker introduced the President.

The President spoke as follows :

Fellow Citizens:—I am here again surprised and very deeply touched by this outpouring of my fellow-citizens and by the deep and respectful interest which you have taken in us.   I cannot find words to express the delight which we have felt as we observed the beauty and, more than all, the comfort and prosperity which characterizes the great state of California.

Everywhere we have been received with the most kindly expression, and everywhere surprise has been in ambush to excite our wondering admiration

I am glad to observe here, as I have elsewhere, that my old comrades have turned out to witness afresh, by this demonstration, their love of the flag and their vener- ation for our American institutions.   My comrades, I greet you every one to-day.   I doubt not that I see before

me representatives of the army from all of the States that
made contribution to that great armed force that subdued
rebellion and brought home the flag in honor and in
triumph. I hope you have found on this flowery and
prosperous land and the happy home you have built up
here, and the wives and children that graced your fireside,
a sweet contrast to those times of peril and hardship which
you have experienced in the army, and I trust, above all,
that under these genial and kindly influences you still
maintain that devotion to our institutions, and are teach-
ing it to your children, whom you are bringing up to
take our places, if it should be our sad fortune ever again
to be involved in strife.

We often speak of our children stepping in the footsteps of our fathers; but I saw, a year ago in Boston, at
the great review of the Grand Army of the Republic,
thousands and thousands of veterans, aged and stricken
down with labor, who had passed by me with the same
springy step that characterized you when you carried
the flag from your home. So we will have to
leave this and the next generation to come to take
our place, knowing in their hands our institutions are
safe, and in their hands the honor and the glory of the
flag will be maintained, and we may quietly go to our
rest with God so long as we are true to ourselves, and
that our children will make any sacrifice for the flag will
manifest itself upon the proper occasion and at any cost.

Now, I thank you again most kindly for your friendly

interest, and I must beg you to excuse any further speech making, as we must journey on to other scenes like this. Good-bye and God bless you, comrades.

MONTEREY, CALIFORNIA.

APRIL 30.

The Presidential party, with the invited guests, were met at the Hotel del Monte by Dr. Westfall, C. I. Burks and J. T. Stockwell, members of the Monterey reception committee. The procession of carriages, arrayed in bunting drove to the old Capitol, now a schoolhouse. The whole populace was assembled in the green square as the President came in sight, bells were rung and the people filled the air with shouts. Mayor Hill delivered an eloquent address of welcome. He spoke of the town's history and its venerable associations, honored not alone in California, but throughout the Union.

As a souvenir of the occasion, on behalf of the citizens of Monterey, Mayor Hill presented the President with a beautiful silver card in a plush case. It had etched on it a miniature picture of the old Monterey Custom-house. In quaint script was lettered the following:

"Old Custom-house, where the American flag was first raised in California, July 7, 1846. Monterey, April 30, 1891. Greeting to our President."

President Harrison's address bore a local coloring, which seemed to inspire him with apt sentiment. He spoke as follows:

"*Mr. Mayor and Fellow-Citizens:*" Our whole pathway through the State of California has been paved with good-will. We have been made to walk upon flowers. Our hearts have been touched and refreshed at every point by the voluntary offerings of your hospitable people. Our trip has been one continual ovation of friendliness. I have had occasion to say before that no man is entitled to appropriate to himself these tributes. They witness a peculiar characteristic of the American people. Unlike many other people less happy, we give our devotion to a Government, to its Constitution, to its flag, and not to men. We reverence and obey those who have been placed by our own suffrages and choice in public stations, but our allegiance, our affection, is given to our beneficient institutions, and upon this rock our security is based. We are not subject to those turbulent uprisings that prevail where the people follow leaders rather than institutions; where they are caught by the glamour and dash of brilliant men rather than by the steady law of free institutions.

I rejoice to be for a moment among you this morning. The history of this city starts a train of reflections in my mind that I cannot follow out in speech, but the impression of them will remain with me as long as I live. [Applause.] California and its coast was essential to the integrity and completeness of the American Union. But who can tell what may be the result of the establishment here of free institutions, the setting up by the wisdom and foresight and courage of the early pioneers in California of a commonwealth that was very early received into the American Union. We see to-day what has been wrought. But who can tell what another century will disclose, when these valleys have become thick with a prosperous and thriving and happy people. I thank you again for your cordial greeting and bid you good morning. [Cheers.]

SANTA CRUZ, CALIFORNIA.

MAY 1.

Mayor Bowman presented the President who made the following response.

Mr. Mayor and Fellow Citizens:—It seems to me like improvidence that all this tasteful and magnificent display should be but for a moment. In all my journeying in

California, where every city has presented some surprise and where each has been characterized by lavish and generous display, I have not seen anything so suddenly created and yet so beautiful. I am sure we have not ridden through any street more attractive than this. I thank you most sincerely for this cordial welcome. I am sure you are a loyal, and I know you are a loving and kindly people. [Cheers.] We have been received, strangers as we were, with affection, and everywhere, as I look into the faces of this people, I feel my heart swell with pride that I am an American and that California is one of the American states. [Cheers.]

THE BIG TREES.

A short visit was made to these California wonders. The President gazed in awe and admiration at the forest of immense trees into which the train had thundered. President and Mrs. Harrison and twenty-five other members of the party entered the hollow trunk of the great tree once occupied by General Fremont. They could move about within its dark interior with perfect ease. With hands joined thirteen, of the party, including the President, spanned the Giant, one of the largest of the redwoods.

LOS GATOS, CALIFORNIA

MAY 1.

The President received a royal welcome, in which the local militia, Grand Army men, Knights of Pythias and nearly all the inhabitants of the surrounding country participated. He made the following address.

My Fellow Citizens:—If California had lodged a complaint against the last census I should have been inclined to entertain it and to order your people to be counted again. [Laughter.] From what I have seen in these days of pleasant travel through your state, I am sure the census enumerators have not taken you all. We have had another surprise in coming over these mountains, to find that not the valleys alone of California, but its hill tops are capable of productive cultivation. We have been greatly surprised to see vineyards and orchards at these altitudes and to know that your fields rival in productiveness the famous valleys of your state.

I thank you for your cordial greeting. It overpowers me. I feel that these brief stops are but poor recompense for the trouble and care you have taken. I wish we could tarry longer with you. I wish I could know more of you individually, but I can only thank you and say that we will carry away most happy impressions of California, and that in public and in private life it will give me pleasure always to show my appreciation of your great state. [Cheers.]

At the California Institute for the Deaf and Blind.

In response to a short address by C. F. Wilkinson, superintendent, President Harrison said:

It gives me great pleasure to visit these institutions, and I thank you for your welcome. These are institutions of modern civilization, and have been established in all the states. In the early and barbarous ages the afflicted were allowed to suffer neglect and wretchedness. Now you have homes for their comfort and their education. Where affliction has closed one avenue to the mind, science has found a way to open another, and thereby the beauties of nature are revealed. I am sure that gladness has found its way to all these hearts, and that science has found a way for you to have happiness in life. I wish you happiness.

Little Lillie Smith, a blind girl five years of age, then presented the President with a small basket of choice flowers, asking him to accept them on behalf of the children of the institute.

The President bowed in acknowledgment of the gift.

The porch was prettily draped with bunting and flags were numerous, presenting a gay appearance.

President Harrison's carriage turned and he was driven away amid the waving of flags and handkerchiefs of the poor afflicted little children.

SAN FRANCISCO, CALIFORNIA.

MAY 1.

At the Chamber of Commerce, the President of the United States was received by the representatives of the various commercial bodies of the city.

Col. Taylor, president of the Chamber of Commerce, made a speech of some length, touching upon the agricultural wealth of California, and the shipping interests of San Francisco, closing with a warm welcome to the President.

The President made the following reply:

Mr. President and Gentlemen of these assembled Societies:—I have been subjected during my stay in California, in some respects, to the same treatment the policeman accords to the tramp—I have been kept moving on.

[Laughter and applause.] You have substituted flowers and kindness for the policeman's baton. And yet, notwithstanding all this, we come to you this morning not exhausted or used up, but a little fatigued. Your cordial greetings are more exhilerating than your wine, [applause] and perhaps safer for the coustitution. [Laughter and applause.]

I am glad to stand in the presence of this assemblage of business men. I have tried to make this a business administration. [Applause.] Of course we cannot wholly separate politics from a national administration, but I have felt that every public officer owed his best service to the people without distinction of party. [Cries of "Good! good!" and applause]; that in administering official trusts we were in a very strict sense, not merely in a figurative sense, your servants. It has been my desire that in every branch of the public service there should be improvements. I have stimulated all the secretaries and have received stimulus from them in the endeavor, in all the departments of the Government that touch your business life to give you as perfect a service as possible. [Cries of " Good! Good!" and applause.] This we owe to you; but if I were pursuing party ends I should feel that I was by such methods establishing my party in the confidence of the people. [Applause.] I feel that we have come to a point where American industries, American commerce and American influence are to be revived and extended. [Applause.] The American sen-

timent and feeling was never more controlling than now;
and I do not use that term in the narrow sense of native
American, but to embrace all loyal citizens, whether native born or adopted, who have the love of our flag in
their hearts. [Great cheering.] I shall speak to-night,
probably at the banquet of business men, and will not
enter into any lengthy discussion here. Indeed, I am
careful not to trespass upon any forbidden topic, that I
may not in the smallest degree offend those who have
forgotten party politics in extending this greeting to us,
and I do not know how far I should talk upon these public questions. But, since your chairman has alluded to
them, I can say I am in hearty sympathy with the sug-
gestions he has made. [Applause.] I believe there are
methods by which we shall put the American flag upon
the sea again. [Applause.] In speaking the other day
I used an illustration which will perhaps be apt in this
company of merchants. You recall, all of you, certainly
those of my age, the time when no merchant sent out
traveling men. He expected the buyer to come to his
store. Perhaps that was well enough; but certain enterprising men sought custom by putting traveling men with
samples on the road. However the conservative merchant
regarded that innovation, he had but one choice—to put
traveling men on the road or go out of business. In this
question of shipping we are in a similar condition. The
great commercial governments of the world have stimulated their shipping interest by direct or indirect subsidies,

while we have been saying, "No, we prefer the old way."
We must advance or—I will not say go out of business, for
we have already gone out. [Applause.] I thank you
most cordially for your greeting, and bid you good-by.
[Applause.]

AT THE PAVILION.

MAY I.

The President and party were escorted to
the Mechanics Pavilion by a detail of mounted
police and the three regiments of the 2d Brigade
of the California National Guard.

No heartier reception was accorded the President on the Pacific coast than that at the
Pavilion, where he spoke to hundreds of
veterans of the civil war, gazed into the faces
of thousands of school children and was cheered
by thousands of citizens.

Comrades of the Grand Army of the Republic:—It will
not be possible in so large a hall for me to make myself
heard, and yet I cannot refuse when appealed to to say
a word of kindly greeting to those comrades who have
found their homes on the Pacific coast. I have no doubt
that all the loyal States of the Union are represented in
this assembly, and it is a pleasure to know that after the

strife and hardships of those years of battle you have
found among the flowers and fruits of the earth, homes
that are full of pleasantness and peace.

It was that these things might continue to be that
you went to battle ; it was that these homes might be
preserved ; it was that the flag and all it symbolizes
might be perpetuated that you fought and many of our
comrades died. All this land calls you blessed. The
fruits of division and strife that would have been ours if
secession had succeeded, would have been full of bitter-
ness. The end that was attained by your valor under
the providence of God has brought peace and prosperity
to all the States. [Applause.]

It gave me great pleasure in passing through the
Southern States to see how your work had contributed
to their prosperity. No man can look upon any of these
States through which we campaigned and fought without
realizing that what seemed to their people a disaster was,
under God, the opening of a great gate of prosperity and
happiness. [Applause.]

All those fires of industry which I saw through the
south were lighted at the funeral pyre of slavery. [Cries
of " Good," " Good" and applause.] They were impossible under the conditions that existed previously in
those States. We are now a homogeneous people. You,
in California, full of pride and satisfaction with the greatness of your State will always set above it the greater
glory and the greater citizenship which our flag symbol-

izes. [Cheers.] You went into the war for the defense
of the Union; you have come out to make your contribution to the industries and progress of this age of peace.
As, in our States of the Northwest, the winter covering
of snow hides and warms the vegetation, and, with the
coming of the spring sun, melts and sinks into the earth
to refresh the root, so this great army was a covering and
defense, and, when the war was ended, turned into rivulets
of refreshment to all the pursuits of peace. [Applause.]
There was nothing greater in all the world's story than
the assembling of this army except its disbandment.
[Applause.] It was an army of citizens: and, when the
war was over, the soldier was not left at the tavern—he
had a fireside towards which his steps hastened. He
ceased to be a soldier and became a citizen. [Cheers.]

I observe, as I look into your faces, that the youth of
the army must have settled on the Pacific coast. [Laugh-
ter and applause.] You are younger men here than we
are in the habit of meeting at our Grand Army post in
the East. May all prosperity attend you; may you be
able to show yourselves in civil life, as in the war, the
steadfast, unfaltering, devoted friends of this flag you
are willing to die for. [Great cheering.]

When the military review and reception at
the Pavilion closed the President was driven to
the Palace Hotel, where the ladies and other
members of the party had preceded him.

The ingenuity of the florist had converted the
hotel into a wonderful flower show—from striking
decorations in the court yard to the exquisitely ap-
pointed rooms of the President and Mrs. Harrison. Some of the most beautiful floral pieces
ever made in this city were placed here, the
largest, a gift to Mrs. Harrison, being a bed of
La France roses 5 feet in diameter. Above it
were two horns of plenty, made of pansies and
roses. Surrounding the whole was a huge crown
of La France roses.

THE BANQUET.

MAY 1.

At the banquet in honor of President Harrison there was a large representation of the
business, professional, political, educational and
society circles of this city. Of all the entertain-
ments extended to the President and his party
on the Pacific coast, the banquet was probably
one of the most select.

After the dinner and when the dessert and
champagne were announced by the bill of fare,
General Barnes arose and introduced the Presi-

dent in a neat speech. The President answered as follows:

Mr. President and Gentlemen:—When the Queen of Sheba visited the court of Solomon and saw its splendors she was compelled to testify that the half had not been told her. Undoubtedly the emissaries of Solomon's court who had penetrated to her distant territory found themselves in a like situation to that which attends Californians when they travel East; they are afraid too much to put to test the credulity of their hearers. [Laughter applause.] And as a gentleman of your state said to me, it has resulted in a prevailing indisposition among Californians to tell the truth out of California. [Laughter and applause.] Not all because Californians are unfriendly to the truth, [Laughter.] but solely out of compassion to their hearers. [Laughter.] They address themselves to the capacity of those who hear them, [Laughter.] and, taking warning by the fate of the man who told a sovereign of the Indies that he had seen water so solid that it could be walked upon, they do not carry their best stories away from home. [Laughter.]

It has been, much as I have seen of California, a brilliant delusion to me and to those who have journeyed with me. The half had not been told of the productiveness of your valleys, of the blossoming orchards, of the gardens laden with flowers. We have seen and been entranced. Our pathway has been strewn with flowers.

We have been surprised when we were in a region of orchards and roses to be suddenly pulled up to a station and asked to address some remarks to a pyramid of pig tin. [Laughter and applause.] Products of the mine, rare and exceptional, have been added to the products of the field until the impression has been made upon my mind that if any new want should be developed in the arts, possibly if any want should be developed in statesmanship, or any vacancies in office, [Great laughter.] we have a safe reservoir that can be drawn upon ad libitum. [Laughter and applause.]

But my friends, sweeter than all the incense of flowers, richer than all the products of mines, has been the gracious, unaffected and hearty kindness with which the people of California have everywhere received us]great applause]—without division, without dissent, a simple and yet magnificent American welcome. [Great applause.]

It is gratifying that it should be so. We may carry into our campaigns, into our conventions and congresses, discussions and divisions; but how grand it is that we are a people who bow reverently to the decision when it is rendered, and who will follow the flag everywhere, always and with entire devotion of heart, without asking what party may have furnished the leader in whose hands it is placed. [Enthusiastic cheering.]

I believe we have come to a new epoch as a nation. There are opening portals before us, inviting us to enter, opening portals to trade and influence and prestige such as we have never seen before. [Great applause.]

We will pursue the paths of peace. We are not a warlike nation. All our instincts, all our history is in the lines of peace. [Applause.] Only intolerable aggression, only the peril of our institutions or the flag can thoroughly arouse us. [Great applause.]

With capabilities for war, on land or sea, unexcelled by any nation in the world, we are smitten with the love of peace. [Applause.]

We would promote the peace of this hemisphere by placing judiciously some large guns about the Golden Gate [great and enthusiastic cheering] simply for saluting purposes [laughter and cheers], and yet they should be of the best modern type. [Cheers.]

We should have on the sea some good vessels. We don't need as great a navy as some other people, but we do need a sufficient navy of first class ships simply to make sure that the peace of the hemisphere is preserved [cheers], simply that we may not leave the great distant marts of commerce and our few citizens who may be domiciled there to feel lonesome for the sight of the American flag. [Cheers.]

We are making fine progress in the construction of the navy. The best English constructors have testified to the completeness and perfection of some of our latest ships. It is a source of great gratification to me that here in San Francisco the energy, enterprise and courage of

some of your citizens have constructed a plant capable
of building the best modern ships. [Cries of "Good!
good!" and cheers.] I saw with great delight the magnificent launch of one of these new vessels. I hope that
you may so enlarge your capacities for construction that
it will not be necessary to send any naval vessel around
the Horn. [Cheers.]

We want merchant ships. [Cheers.] I believe we
have come to a time when we should choose whether we
will continue to be non-participants in the commerce of
the world or will now vigorously, with the push and
energy which our people have shown in other lines of
enterprise, claim our share of the world's commerce.
[Cheers.]

I will not enter into the discussion of methods. The
Postal bill of the last session of Congress makes a beginning. Here in California, where, for so long a time, a
postal service that did not pay its own way was maintained by the Government, where for other years the
Government has maintained mail lines into your valleys,
reaching out to every remote community and paying out
yearly a hundred times the revenue that was derived, it
ought not to be difficult to persuade you that our ocean
mail should not longer be the only service for which we
refuse to expend even the revenues derived from it.
[Cheers.]

It is my belief that under the operation of the law to
which I have referred we shall be able to stimulate ship

building to secure some new lines of American steamships and to increase the ports of call of those now established. [Enthusiastic cheering.]

It will be my first effort to do what may be done under the powers lodged in me by the law to open and
increase trade with the counties of Central and South
America. [Cheers.] I hope it may not be long. I know
it will not be long if we but unitedly pursue this great
scheme until one can take a sail in the bay of San Francisco and see some deepwater ships come in bearing our
own flag. [Enthusiastic and continued cheering.]

During our excursion the other day I saw three great
vessels come in; one carried the Hiwaiian flag and two
the English flag.

I am a thorough believer in the Nicaragua canal.
[Cheers.] You have pleased me so much that I would
like a shorter water communication between my state
and yours. [Cheers.] Influences and operations are
now started that will complete, I am sure, this stately
enterprise.

But, my fellow-citizens, and Mr. President, this is the
fifth time this day that I have talked to gatherings of
California friends, and we have so much taxed the hospitality of San Francisco [cries of " No, no!"] in making
our arrangements to make this city the center of a whole
week's sight seeing, that I do not want to add to your
other burdens the infliction of a longer speech. [cries
of "Go on!"]

Right royally have you welcomed us with all that is
rich and prodigal in provisions and display, with all gen-
erousness and friendliness. I leave my heart with you
when I go. [Great and prolonged cheering.]

SACRAMENTO, CALIFORNIA.

MAY 2.

Mayor Comstock presented Gov. Markham
who delivered the address of welcome.

WELCOME TO THE EXECUTIVE.

He said, addressing the President: At almost the
close of your visit to our State, it is again my pleasant
duty to meet and welcome you. * * * * * * *

Mr. President, you now stand upon historic ground.
Within the limits of this city are the crumbling ruins of
Sutter's Fort, where that generous old pioneer dispensed
hospitality with a lavish hand, reigned like a feudal lord,
and gave to all new comers a hearty and hospitable welcome after their dangerous and toilsome journey of
months, which was required to reach the Pacific shores.
It is but a step to the spot where the discovery of gold
was made, an event which has had more influence, perhaps, upon the commerce and progress of our country
than any material event since the great Columbus
crossed the supposed impassable ocean. The discovery

of gold at Coloma has furnished the life-blood of commerce, giving impetus to enterprises without a parallel
and more than doubled the value of all the property of
the republic.

I find it much easier, Mr. President, to say greetings
than farewells, but I assure you that you depart with the
prayers of our people for your safe return, and their good
wishes for your future prosperity.

"As President Harrison stood upon the
elevated platform in front of the Capitol building and looked down upon and over the vast
sea of human faces that were upturned to his
with so much respect and admiration expressed
thereon, he would have been less than human
if his heart did not respond to such a greeting.
Standing there in the soft atmosphere of a perfect California spring morning, in the presence
of from twelve to fifteen thousand people, representing every element in the community;
looking out upon the tree-embowered streets
and happy homes that surrounded him; upon
the hundreds of prettily dressed school children
who waved their little flags at him, and who had
just strewn his pathway with roses almost knee-
deep—it is no wonder the President paused in his

remarks, and said there was no person so gifted
of tongue as to be able to give fitting expression to the thoughts and feelings that thrilled
his brain and heart at that moment.

It was one of those events that occur so
rarely within the average limit of a lifetime,
when one feels that words are meaningless, and
that the eloquence of silence alone can do
justice to the grandeur and sublimity of the
occasion. Everyone who stood within sight of
the President as he gazed in silence at the
charming and animated picture spread out before him, could read in his face that his heart
was full of gratitude and pride—that he fully
appreciated the people's patriotism and respect
for the high office he represented, and that he
was proud to know that here, on the far away
sunset slopes of the continent, the people are
all Americans—all happy, prosperous, contented, and loyal to their country."

THE PRESIDENT'S SPEECH.

Governor Markham and Fellow Citizens:—Our eyes
have rested upon no more beautiful or impressive sight
since we entered California. This fresh delightful morn-

ing; this vast assemblage of contented and happy people; this impressive building, dedicated to the uses of civil Government—all things to us—tend to inspire our hearts with pride and with gratitude.

Gratitude to that overruling Providence that turned hither, after the discovery of this continent, the steps of those who had the capacity to organize a free and a representative government; gratitude for that Providence that has developed those feeble colonies and the inhospitable coast into these millions of prosperous people, who have found another sea and bordered its sunny shores with a happy and a growing people. [Applause.] Gratitude to that Providence that led us through civil strife to glory, and to a perfection of unity as people that was not otherwise possible. Gratitude, that we have to-day a union of free States, without a slave to stand as a rebuke and a reproach to that immortal dec_laration upon which our Government rests. [Applause.] Pride, that our people have achieved so much; that these early pioneers who struggled in the face of discouragement and difficulties more appalling than those that met Columbus when he turned the prows of his little vessels towards an unknown shore—the perils of starvation, the perils of savage Indians, the perils of sickness—and yet triumphing over all these difficulties, they burst out upon this sunny slope of the Pacific, to set up here the starry banner and to establish civil institutions. [Applause.] Every Californian who has fol-

lowed in their footsteps, every man and woman who is
to-day enjoying the harvest of their brave endeavor,
should always lift his hat to a pioneer of 1849. [Ap-
plause.]

We stand here at the political center of a great State,
at this building where your law-makers assemble, chosen
by your suffrages to execute your will in framing those
rules of conduct which shall control the life of the citizen.
May you always find here patriotic and conscientious
men to do your work; may they always assemble here
with a high sense of duty to this brave, intelligent and
honorable people; may they catch the great lesson of
our Government, that our people need only such regula-
tions as shall restrain the ill-disposed, and which will
give the largest liberty to individual enterprise and effort.
[Applause.]

May all blessings attend you. No man is gifted with
speech to describe the beauty and the impressiveness of
this great occasion. I am awed in this presence. I bow
reverentially to this great assemblage of free, intelligent
and enterprising American sovereigns. [Applause.]

Now we must bid you farewell. I am glad to have
had this hasty glympse of this earliest center of immigration and enterprise. I am glad to stand in the locality
where that memorable event, the discovery of gold, trans-
pired; and yet, after you have washed your sand for gold,
after the eager rush for sudden wealth, after all these,
you have come into a richer heritage, into the possession

of those fields, in these enduring and inexhaustible treasures of your soil which will perpetually sustain a great population.

Again, and in parting, sir, to you, the representative of this people, I give the most hearty thanks of all these journeying with me and mine, for the kindly and continuous, yea, even affectionate attention which have followed us in all our footsteps through California.

SACRAMENTO'S SOUVENIR.

Ex-Governor Booth presented the Executive with a handsome souvenir on behalf of the people of Sacramento. It consists of a massive gold disc which bears the seal of the city on one side, and on the other the following inscription :

> *Compliments of*
> *The Citizens of Sacramento to*
> *PRESIDENT AND MRS. HARRISON,*
> *On the Occasion of their Visit,*
> *May second,*
> *eighteen hundred ninety-one.*

BENICIA, CALIFORNIA.
MAY 2.

The President's special train stopped a few minutes at Benicia, and a floral tribute in the shape of a cannon was presented to the President by the school children, who were drawn up in a body. In excepting the flowers the President said:

My Friends:—I thank you most sincerely for this pleasant tribute which I have received from these children. It is a curious thing perhaps that among the earliest names that became familiar to me in my younger days was Benicia. In 1857, when the United States sent an armed expedition to Utah, and thence across the continent, I happened to have an elder and much beloved brother who was a lieutenant in that campagne. He was stationed at Benicia barracks, and his letters from this place have fixed it in my memory and recall to me, as I stand here this morning, very tender memories of one who has long since gone to his rest. I thank you again for this demonstration.

SAN FRANCISCO.
MAY 2.

A grand reception was given to President Harrison and his party in the club-house of the

Union League in the evening. It was no doubt as hearty and cordial as any he has been tendered, and will doubtless remember the pleasant affair as being one of the most, if not the most, notable of any in which he has taken part since his arrival upon the Pacific coast.

The reception over, Samuel Shortridge stepped before the President and in a short address presented him a souvenir, gold plate six by four inches in size, bearing a fac-simile of the invitation. In the lower left-hand corner was the great seal of the State worked in various colors of gold and underneath the seal, which was raised, was a standard and an American flag in enameled colors.

The President accepted the souvenir with a bow, and said :

California is full of ambuscades, not hostile, but with all the embarrassments that attend surprise. In hasty driving this afternoon, when I thought I was to visit Oakland, I was suddenly drawn up in front of a college and asked to make an address. A moment afterward I was before an assylum for deaf, dumb and blind, the character of which I did not know until the carriage stopped in front of it. All this taxes the ingenuity, as your kindness moves the heart of one who is making a hurried journey through California.

I do not need such souvenirs as this to keep fresh in my heart this visit to your State. It will be pleasant, however, to show to others who have not participated in this enjoyment—this record of a trip that has been very eventful, and one of perpetual sunshine and happiness. I do not think I could have endured the labor and toil of travel unless I had been borne up by the inspiriting and hearty good will of your people. I do not know what collapse is in store for me when it is withdrawn. I fear I shall need a vigorous tonic to keep up to the high level of enjoyment and inspiration which your kind treatment has given me.

I thank you for this pleasant social enjoyment and this souvenir of it.

RED BLUFF, CALIFORNIA.
MAY 4.

A large crowd assembled at the station and gave the President a most enthusiastic welcome. Capt. Matlock, an old army comrade, introduced the President to the people. President Harrison in his speech referred to Capt. Matlock, and to a number of Indiana people whom he had met in this state. Continuing he said:

My Friends:—You have a most beautiful state, capable of promoting the comfort of your citizens in a very high degree, and although already occupying a high place in the galaxy of states, it will, I am sure, take a much higher one. It is pleasant to see how the American spirit prevails among all your people, love for the flag and its constitution, those settled and permanent things that live wherever man go or come. They come to us from our fathers and will pass down to our children. You are blessed with a genial climate and most productive soil. I see you have in this northern part of California what I have seen elsewhere, a well ordered community, with churches and schools, which indicates that you are not giving all your thoughts to material things, but are thinking of those things that qualify the soul for the hereafter. We have been treated to another surprise this morning in the first shower we have seen in California. I congratulate you that it rained here. May all the blessings fall on you like this gentle rain. [Cheers.]

REDDING, CALIFORNIA.
MAY 4.

Showers of flowers and a national salute greeted the President. He spoke as follows:

Fellow Citizens:—It is very pleasant as we near the northern line of California, after having traveled the val-

leys of the south, and are soon to leave the state in
which we have had so much pleasurable intercourse with
its people, to see, as I have seen here, a multitude of contented, prosperous and happy people.   I am assured that
you are here a homogeneous people, Americans by birth
or by free choice, lovers of one flag, one constitution.
[Cheers.]

It seems to me, as I look into the faces of these California audiences, that life must be easier here than it is
in the East   I see absolutely no evidence of want. Every
one seems to be well nourished.   Your appearance gives
evidence that the family board is well supplied, and the
gladness on your faces is evidence that in your social relations everything is quiet, orderly and hopeful.   I thank
you for your friendly demonstrations.   I wish it were
possible for me to do more in exchange for all your great
kindness than simply to say thank you.   But I do fondly
thank you, and shall carry away from your state the very
happiest impressions and the very pleasantest memories.
[Cheers.]

MEDFORD, OREGON.

MAY 5.

The visit to Medford was acknowledged by
a general illumination of the town, bonfires being particularly numerous.   The President was

introduced to the throng by the Mayor of Medford, and made the following speech :

Comrades and Fellow Citizens:—It gives me great pleasure to see you to-night, especially to these old comrades' greeting. I would have you think me as a comrade. I recall those army scenes which are fresh in your minds as well—the scenes of privation, suffering and battle—and I am glad to see that the old flag you took to the field and brought home in honor is still held in honor among you. It is a beautiful emblem of a great Government. We ought to teach our children to love it and to regard it as a sacred thing—a thing for which men have died and for which men will die. It symbolizes the government of the states under one constitution, for while you are all Oregonians as I am an Indianian, and each has his pride in State institutions, and all that properly pertains to our Stategovernment, we have a larger and greater pride in the fact that we are citizens of a nation, of a union of states having a common constitution. It is this flag that represents us on the sea and in foreign countries; it is under this flag that our navies sail and our armies march. I thank you for this cordial greeting. I hope you have found in this state comfortable homes, and that in the years that remain to you, God will follow you with those blessings which your courage and patriotism and sacrifices have so well merited. [Cheers.]

ALBANY, OREGON.

MAY 5.

The cadets of the State Agricultural college at Corvallis, twelve miles distant, were drawn up in line at the station and formed part of the reception committee. There was a fine display of flags and a profusion of floral tributes. Mayor J. L. Cowan introduced the president to the throng. President Harrison acknowledged their cheers with the following address:

My Fellow Citizens:—It gives me great pleasure to see you, and to have the testimony of your presence here this wet morning to the interest you take in this little party of strangers that are pausing only for a moment in your midst. We do not need any assurance, as we look over an American audience like this, that upon some things, at least, we are of one mind. One of these things is that we have a union indissoluble; that we have a flag we all honor and that shall suffer no dishonor from any quarter. While I regret the inclemency of the morning, I have been thinking that after all there was a sort of instructive moral force in the uncertainty of the weather, which our friends in Southern California do not enjoy. How can a boy or young woman be well trained in self denial and resignation who does not know what it is to have a picnic or a picnic dress spoiled by a shower, or some fishing excursion by a storm? I thank you for this welcome.

SALEM, OREGON.

MAY 5.

The Presidential party were driven to the Capitol where addresses were delivered by Governor Pennoyer, bidding the President welcome to Oregon, and by Mayor D'Arcy in behalf of Salem. The President made the following response:

Governor Pennoyer, Mr. Mayor, and Fellow Citizens: —It is very pleasant to be assured by these kindly words which have been spoken by the chief officer of this municipality that we are welcome to the state of Oregon and to the city of Salem.

I find here, as I have found elsewhere, that these cordial words of welcome are repeated with increased emphasis by the kindly faces of those who assemble to greet us I am glad that here, as elsewhere, we look into the faces of happy, prosperous, contented, liberty-loving, patriotic, American citizen. [Applause.]

The wholesome and just division of power between the three great independent co-ordinate branches of

government—executive, legislative, and judicial—have
already demonstrated that what seems to the nations of
Europe to be a complicated and jangling system, produces
in fact the most perfect harmony, and the most complete
and satisfactory organization for social order and for national strength.

We stand here today in one of these halls set apart
to the law-making power of your state ; those who assemble here are chosen by your suffrages—they come here
as representatives to enact into law those views of public questions which have met the sanction of a majority
of your people, expressed in an orderly and honest way
at your ballot boxes. I hope it may be alway found to
be true of Oregon that your legislative body is a representative body, that coming from the people its service
is consecrated to the people, and the purpose of its creation is attained by leaving the well-ordered and well disposed the largest liberty, by curbing by wholesome laws
the ill-disposed and the lawless, and providing by economical methods for the public need. The judiciary, that
comes next in our system, to interpret and to apply the
public statute, has been, in our country, a safe refuge for
all who are oppressed, a wise tribunal for the decision of
all public questions, and it is greatly to our credit as a
nation that with rare exceptions those who have worn
the judicial ermine, the high tribunals of our country,
and notably the supreme court of the United States, have
continued to retain the confidence of the people of the

whole country. The duty of the executive is to administer law; the power of the militia is lodged with him. He does not frame statutes, though in most states and under our national government a veto power is lodged in him with a view to require reconsideration of any particular measure. But a public executive has one plain duty; it is to enforce all laws, with kindness and prudence, but with promptness and with inexorable decision [prolonged applause.] He cannot choose what laws he will enforce any more than the citizen will choose what laws he will obey. It is the law, having passed through those constitutional forms which are necessary to make it binding upon the people, and that king, all men must obey [applause.] It is a great pleasure to find so general a disposition everywhere to obey the law. I have but one message for the North or for the South, the East or West, as I journey through this land—it is to hold up the law [applause] and to say everywhere that every man owes an allegiance to it, and that all law-breakers must be left to the deliberate and quiet and safe disposition of an established tribunal. [Applause,]

You are well proud of your great state. Its capabilities are numerous; its adaptations to comfortable life are peculiar and fine, and years will bring you increased population and increased wealth. I hope they will bring with them, marching in this state of progress of material things, those finer things—education, piety, respect for the law, pure homes and orderly lives [applause]; but

over all this matter of state pride—over all our rejoicing
in the facilities of life which are about us in our respective states, we look with greater pride to that great arch of
government that unites these states and makes of them
all one great nation.   [Prolonged applause.]

But, my fellow citizens, the difficulties which I already
see interposed between us and a train which is scheduled
to depart very soon—difficulties growing out of your
friendliness, warm me to bring these remarks to a speedy
close.   I beg again, most profoundly, to thank you   for
this evidence of your respect—for this evidence of your
love for the institutions of our common country.   [Pro-
longed applause and cheering.]

PORTLAND, OREGON.

MAY 5.

Notwithstanding the wet and disagreeable
weather on the arrival of the Presidential train
the splendid procession under command of Col.
T. M. Anderson, U. S. A., consisting of the
Fourteenth Regulars, Infantry and Artillery of
the Oregon National Guard, G. A. R., Civic
Societies and four hundred school children were
reviewed by the President.   At the Exposition
building in the evening, Mayor Mack DeLush-

mutt in a speech of welcome presented the President to an audience of upwards of fifteen thous-
and citizens of Portland.

The President's speech :

Mr. Mayor and Fellow Citizens:—No more brilliant or
inspiring scene than this has been presented to our eyes
in this wonderful series of receptions which have been
extended to us on our journey. You have been filled
with regret to-day that your weeping skies did not present to us the fair spectacle which you had hoped ; and
yet this very discouragement has but added to the glory
of this magnificent reception. [Cheers.] To stand in
the bright sunshine of a genial day and to wave a welcome is not so strong a proof of the affectionate interest
of a people as you have given to-day standing in this
down-pouring rain. [Cheers.] In the presence of a
multitude like this, in a scene made brilliant by these
decorations, I stand inadequate to any suitable expression of the gratitude that fills my heart. [Cheers.]

I was quite inclined to stand by the superintendent of
the census in the count which he made of the states ;
but I am afraid if I had witnessed this scene, pending
your application for a recount, that it would have been
granted. [Laughter and great cheering.] I am sorry
that it could not have been made, as the people turned
out to give us this welcome; I am sure no one would
have been missed. [Laughter and cheers.]

This state is interesting in its history; the establishment of the authority of the United States over this
region was an important event in our national history.
The possession of the Columbia and of Puget sound was
essential to the completeness and the roundness of our
empire. We have here in this belt of states, reaching
from the gulf of California to the straits of Fuca, a magnificent possession which we could not have dispensed
with at all. [Cheers.] The remoteness of Oregon from the
older settled states, the peril and privation which attended
the steps of the pioneer as he came hither delayed the development of this great country. You are now but beginning to realize the advantages of closer and easier communications. You are but now beginning to receive from an
impartial and beneficient government that attention
which you well deserve. [Cheers.]

That this river of yours should be made safe and
deep, so that waiting commerce may come without
obstruction to your wharf, is to be desired. [Cheers.]
It should receive those appropriations which are necessary to make the work accomplish the purpose in view.
[Cheers.] I believe that you may anticipate a largely
increased commerce. Looking out as you do towards
the regions across the Pacific it would be but natural
that this important center should draw from them and
exchange with them a great and increasing commerce.
[Cheers.] I am in entire sympathy with the suggestion
of the mayor that this commerce should be carried in

American ships. [Cheers.] A few days ago, when I sailed in the harbor of San Francisco, I saw three great deep-water ships come into that port. One carried the flag of Hawaii and two the English flag. None bore at the masthead the stars and stripes: I believe it is the duty of the national government to take such steps as will restore the American merchant marine. [Cheers.] Why shall we not have our share in the great commerce of the world? I cannot but believe—and such inspiring presence as this but kindle and confirm my belief—that we are come to a time when this nation should look to the future and step forward bravely and courageously in new lines of enterprise. [Cheers.]

The Nicaragua canal should be completed. [Cheers.] Our harbors should have adequate defense. [Cheers.] We should have upon the sea a navy of first-class ships. [Cheers.] We are here in the most kindly relations to these South American and Central American countries. We have been content that Europe should do the commerce of these nations. We have not availed ourselves of the advantages of neighborhood and of friendly kindred republican institutions to develope our commerce with those people. We have fortunately, as a result of the great conference of American nations, set on foot measures that I confidently hope will bring to us speedily our just share of this great commerce. [Cheers.]

I am glad to know that we are here to-night as American citizens, lovers of the one flag and the one consti-

tution. [Enthusiastic cheering.]   Proud   of   Oregon!
Yes, you may well be proud of Oregon.   But, my countrymen, above all, crowning all, greater than all, is our
American citizenship. [Great cheering.]   What would
one of these States be without the other?   What is it
that gives us prestige abroad and power at home?   It is
that we have formed a government of the people ; that
we have one flag and speak with one voice to all the
nations of the earth. [Enthusiastic cheering.]   I hope
that narrow sentiment that regards the authority of the
United States or its officers as alien or strange, has once
and forever been extinguished in this land of ours
[Great cheering.]   Again I assure you that you have
given us to-day what is to my mind, under the conditions,
taking into account the population of your city, the most
splendid demonstration we have seen on the whole journey.   [Prolonged and enthusiastic cheering.]

TACOMA, WASHINGTON.

MAY 6.

A more unpleasant May day, from a wild
torrent to a light shower, could not have been
experienced than that which greeted the President's party on their arrival in Washington.
Nevertheless the streets were thronged with the
populace.

Gov. Ferry, as the Chief Executive, bade the President welcome, and Gen. John W. Sprague welcomed him in a short speech.

President Harrison responded:

My Fellow Citizens.—I feel that it would be cruel to prolong this exposure which you are enduring in the inclement weather of the day. I visited your city and the region of Puget sound six years ago. I found this country then enveloped in smoke so that these grand mountain tops, of which mention has been made in the address of welcome, were hidden from our view. I come again and the smoke is replaced by fog, and we are still, I suppose, to take the existence of these snow-clad peaks on faith. [Laughter and applause.] I don't know but there is a benevolent provision for your comfort in the fact that this magnificent scenery, this unmatched body of water are frequently hidden from the eye of the traveler. If everyone who journeys hither could see it all, everybody would want to live here, and there wouldn't be room. [Laughter and cheers.] I congratulate you, citizens of Tacoma, upon the magnificent, almost magical transformation which has been wrought here in these six years since I last saw your city. It has been amazing; it is a tribute to the energy and the enterprise and courage of your people that will endure and increase, and attract in a yet higher degree the attention of the whole country. A harbor like this, so safe and commodious, and deep, upon Puget Sound, should be made to bear a commerce that is but yet in its infancy. I would like to see the prows of some of these great steamship lines entering your ports and carrying the American flag at the masthead. [Cheers.] I believe we have come to the time in our development as a people, when we must step forward with bold progress, or we will lose the advantage we have already attained. We have within ourselves the resources, and a market of which the world is envious. We have been content, in the years gone by, to allow other nations to do the carrying trade of the world. We have been content to see the markets of these American Republics lying south of us, mastered and controlled by European nations. I think the period of discontent with these things has now come to our people, and I believe the time is auspicious for the enlargment of our commerce with these friendly Republics lying to the south of us. I believe the time propitious for re-establishing upon the sea the American merchant marine, that shall do its share of the carrying trade of the world. [Applause.]

My friends, I desire to again express to you my regret that to give us this magnificent welcome, under circumstances so inauspicious, you have been exposed to so much wet. I especially regretted, as I passed those long lines of mere school children, that they should have been exposed in order to do us honor. I will not detain you longer. For your city, for this magnificent young state that we have received into the great sisterhood of the

Union, of which you are a glorious part, we give our aspirations, our prayers and our best endeavors. [Applause.]

SEATTLE, WASHINGTON.

MAY 6.

The presidential party made a trip from Tacoma to Seattle by boat, being welcomed aboard the palatial steamer, the city of Seattle, at Tacoma, at 11 a. m. Elliott Bay was covered with vessels and boats of every description. The reception by the Seattle committee aboard the steamer was without formality, save a few remarks by Mayor White, to which the President responded:

Mr. Mayor: I accept with great gratitude the words of welcome on behalf of the citizens of Seattle. It will give me a great deal of pleasure to contrast my observations of your State in 1890 with what we see to-day. I have not lost track of the progress of Seattle, but have, through friends, been advised of the marvelous development which you have made—how you have repeated, in the substantial character of your edifices, the story of the Chicago fire, coming out of what seemed a disaster with increased magnificence; and finding in it really an advantage. I will defer, until I am in the presence of your people, further acknowledgment of your courtesies, and will now only thank you, as you are repeating what we have observed on our whole trip—the unification of your people and the absoluteness of our sentiment in devotion to our institutions and flag.

"The reception of President Harrison will for many a year be one of the most conspicuous landmarks in Seattle's annals. The enormous outpouring of people, the enthusiasm, the abundance of its decorative display, the grand demonstration in the harbor, and the gathering at the campus will never be forgotten by those who witnessed them. Sunshine might have made the scenes brighter, but the exaltation of popular enthusiasm over all the untoward influences of the weather gave a dignity and impressiveness so the events of the day far beyond the need of adventitious aids and artificial pageantry.

A dense sea of people, estimated at 35,000, gathered around the grand stand on the campus of the University grounds. Mayor White presented Judge Thomas Burke to the President, who delivered the address of welcome. To which President Harrison responded:

Judge Burke and Fellow Citizens: I am sure you have too much kindness in your heart to ask me to make an address to you this afternoon. This chilly air, this drizzling rain, the long exposure during the day which you and these precious children have suffered, warn me, on your account, as well as my own, that I should say but a few words in recognition of this magnificent welcome. Six years ago I visited your beautiful city, and the distinguished gentleman who has been your spokesman to-day was one of a hospitable committee that pointed out to me the beauties of this location. You were then largely a prospective city. Some substantial and promising improvements had been begun, but it was a period of expectancy rather than of realization. I am glad to come to-day and to see how fully and perfectly the large expectations then entertained by your enterprising people have been realized. It is a matter of amazement to look upon these towering substantial granite and iron structures in which the great business of your city is transacted. That disaster, as it seemed to you, which swept away a large portion of the business part of your city, was like the afflictions that come to the saints, a blessing in disguise. [Cheers.] You have done what Chicago did. You have improved the disaster by rearing structures and completing edifices that

were unthought of before. Those who were not enterprising or liberal have been compelled to be liberal and
enterprising in order that they might realize rents for
their property made vacant by fire. [Cheers.] I fully
appreciate the importance of this great body of water
upon which your city is situated. This Sound, this inland sea, must be in the future the highway, the entrepot,
of a great commerce. I do most sincerely believe that
we are entering now upon a new development that will
put the American flag upon the seas and bring to our
ports in American bottoms a largely increased share of
the commerce of the world. [Cheers.] As I have said
in other places, for one I am thoroughly discontented
with the present condition of things. We may differ as
to methods, but I believe the great patriotic heart of our
people is stirred, and that they are bent upon recovering
that share of the world's commerce which we once happily enjoyed. Your demonstration to-day under these
unfavorable environments has been most creditable to
your city. We have certainly seen nothing in a journey
characterized by great demonstrations to surpass this
magnificent scene. [Cheers.] I realize what your spokesman has said, that in all this there is a patriotic expression of the love of our people for the flag and for the
constitution. [Cheers.] And now, my friends, thanking
you for all you have done for me, humbly confessing my
inability to repay you, pledging to you my best efforts to
promote the good of all our people, and that I will have

a watchful observation of the needs of your State, of your harbors, for defense, improvement and security, I bid you good bye. [Cheers.]

THE DALLES, OREGON.
MAY 7.

The President and party left Portland in the morning, and the trip through the picturesque valley of the Columbia was made in the bright sunlight, which disclosed the mountains and cascades in their beauty and grandeur. The first stop of any importance was at The Dalles, where the party received enthusiastic welcome. In responding to the address of welcome by the Mayor the President said:

I quite sympathize with the suggestion of your mayor that it is one of the proper Government functions to improve and open to safe navigation the great waterways of the country. [Cheers.] The Government having reserved to itself the exclusive control of all the navigable inland waters, it is, of course, encumbent upon the Government to see that the people have the best possible use of them. They are important as they furnish cheap transportation and touch the points that are often either for economy or natural reasons inaccessible to railway traffic.

BOISE CITY, IDAHO.
MAY 6.

The President and party passed three hours very pleasantly in this city. The streets were gay with bunting, nearly every building displaying a flag, large or small. The visitors were received at the station by Gov. Wiley, Mayor Pinney, Senator Shoup, Mr. Calvin Cobb, editor of the *Idaho Statesman*, and a general committee.

At the main entrance of the Capitol, Gov. Wiley made an address of welcome on behalf of of the State, and Mayor Finney on behalf of the city.

President Harrison is replying to the addresses of welcome, said:

This is instructive and inspiring to us all as American citizens. It is my great pleasure to stand for a little while this morning in the political capital of this fresh and new State. I had great satisfaction in taking an official part in admitting Idaho to the Union of States. I believe that she was possessed of a population and resources, and capable of a development that fairly entitled her to take her place among the States of the American Union. You are starting now upon a career fo development which I hope and believe will be uninterrupted. Your great mineral resources, now being rapidly developed, have already brought you great wealth. Undoubtedly these are to continue to be sources of enrichment and prosperity to your State, if you do not forget to look at last for that enduring prosperity and increase which our States should have to a development of their agricultural resources. You will, of course, as you have done, carefully guard and serure your political institutions. You will organize them upon a basis of economy and yet at liberal progress. You will take care that only so much revenue is taken from the people as is necessary to the proper public expenditure. [Applause.]

I am glad to see that this banner of liberty, this flag of our fathers, this flag that these, my comrades, here present, defended with honor and brought home with victory from the bloody strife of the civil war, held in honor and estimation among you. [Great applause.] Every man should think of his hat when the starry flag moves by. It symbolizes a free republic, it symbolizes a nation, not an aggregation of states, but one compact, solid government in all its relations to the nations of the earth. [Applause.] Let us always hold it in honor. I am glad to see that it floats, not only over your political capital, but over the schoolhouses of your state. The children should be taught in the primary schools to know the story and to love it. To these young children, entering by the beneficient and early provision of your state into the advantages of that great characteristic American institution, the common school, I give my greeting this morning.   May every good attend them in life and as the cares of life come on to take the place of the joys of childhood, God grant that, instructed in mind and heart, in those things that are high and good, they may bear with honor the responsibility which you will soon lay down.

POCATELLO, IDAHO.

MAY 8.

In response to loud and repeated calls at the reception last night, President Harrison made the following remarks:

Fellow Citizens.—In 1881, that sad summer when General Garfield lay so long in agony, and the people suffered so long in painful suspense, I passed up the Utah and Northern narrow gauge railroad through this place, if it was a place then, to Montana on a visit.   The country through which we have passed is therefore not unfamiliar to me.   I have known of its natural condition and I have seen its capabilities when brought under the stimulating influence of irrigation.   I have had, during my term in the senate as chairman of the committee on territories of that body, to give a good deal of attention to the condition and needs of our territories. My sympathy and interest have always gone out to those who, leaving the settled and populous parts of our country, have pushed the frontiers of civilization further and further to the westward until they have met the Pacific ocean and the setting sun. Pioneers have always been enterprising people. If they had not been they would have remained at home. They endured great hardships and perils in opening these great mines of minerals, which show in your state, and in bringing into subjection these wild plains and making them blossom like gardens. To all such here I would do honor and you should do honor, for they were heroes in the struggle for the subjugation of the untamed country to the uses of man.

I am glad to see that you have here so many happy and prosperous people. I rejoice at the increase of your population and am glad to notice, that with this development in population and material wealth, you are giving attention to those social virtues, to education, and to those influences which sanctify the home, make social order secure, and honor and glorify the institutions of our common country. [Cheers.]

I am glad, not only for the sake of the white man, but of the red man, that these two extensive and useless reservations are being reduced by allotment to the Indians of farms, which they are expected to cultivate and thereby earn their own living. [Cheers.] And unneeded lands shall furnish homes for those who need homes. [Cheers.]

And now, fellow citizens, extending to such comrades of the Grand Army of the Republic as I see scattered about through this audience, my most cordial greeting as a comrade, to these children and these ladies, who shared with you the privations of early life on the frontier, and to all my most cordial greeting and sincere thanks for the kindly demonstration, I will say good-bye. [Great cheers.]

SALT LAKE CITY, UTAH.

MAY 9.

The visitors were taken to the Chamber of Commerce and the President formally opened the building for business. He afterwards reviewed the public school children on East Brigham street and heard them sing "America" and "Hail Columbia." The presidential party then paid a short visit to the Mormon Tabernacle and other points of interest.

The President made the following speech to the school children:

In all this joyous journey through this land of flowers and the sunny South, I have seen nothing more beau-

tiful and inspiring than this scene which has burst upon
us so unexpectedly. This multitude of children bearing
waving banners makes a scene which can never fade
from our memories. Here in the children from the free
schools established and guarded by your public authorities is the hope of Utah and the country. [Cheers.] I
give you my thanks for a demonstration that has cheered
my heart. May each of you enjoy every blessing that a
free country and a beneficent and kindly Creator can
bestow. [Cheers.]

Under escort of a large attachment of the
16th and 21st Regiment of U. S. Infantry, local
military and G. A. R. and Civic societies, the
party were conducted to Liberty Park, where
Governor Thomas delivered an address of welcome and Mayor Geo. M. Scott prefaced his
introduction of the President by a welcoming
speech on behalf of Salt Lake City.

The President responded as follows:

Governor Thomas, Mr. Mayor and Fellow Citizens:
The scene which has been presented to us in this political and commercial center of the Territory of Utah has
been very full of beauty and very full of bright hope.

I have not, in all this long journey, witnessed a scene
of more magnificent welcome or grandeur, or anything

that lifted my heart more than that beautiful picture on
one of your streets this morning, the children from the
public schools of Salt Lake City, waving the one banner
that we all love, and singing the anthem of praise to that
beneficent Providence that led our worthy forefathers to
this land and filled the pathway of this Nation with its
beneficent character until this bright hour.   My service
in public life has been such as to call my special attention and to enlist my special interest in the people of the
Territory of Utah.   It has been a pleasant duty to welcome the Dakotas, Washington, Montana, Idaho and
Wyoming into the great constellation of the States, I
think it has not fallen to any President of the United
States to receive under public law into the Union so large
a number of free States.   The conditions that surround
here in this Territory of a material kind are of the
richest and of the most hopeful character.   The diversity
of your production, of your mines of coal and silver and
iron and lead and gold, placed in such proximity to make
the work of mining and reduction easy and economical.
Your well watered valleys, capable under the skillful
touch of the husbandman, of transformation from barren waste into fruitful fields.   All this lying in easy
touch, and inter-communication, one with the other,
must make the elements of a great political community.
You do not at all need to doubt; you may well step forward with a bold, confident and progressive step in the
development of this great material wealth.   The charac-

teristic of our American institution, the compact of our Government, is that the will of the majority expressed by constitutional and legal methods at the ballot box shall be the supreme law of our community. To the Territories of the United States a measure of local self government has always been given, but the supervisory control of the supreme legislative and executive power has been continuously, as to the Territories, held and exercised by the general Government at Washington. The Territorial state has always been regarded as a temporary one. The Government has always looked forward to a division of that vass domain, first west and northwest of the Ohio, then through the Louisiana purchase, then through these accessions upon the Pacific Coast, and the division of this vast domain into suitable sections, for the establishment of free and independent States. This great progression that has lined the work of creation has gone forward from the Ohio to the Pacific, and now we may journey from Maine to Puget Sound through constituted and established States.

The purification and the purity of the ballot box; those wise provisions, that careful guardianship that shall always make the expression of the will of the people fair, pure and true, is the essential thing in American life. We are a people organized upon principles of liberty, but, my fellow countrymen, it is distinguished from license, it is liberty within and under the law. I have no discord as a public officer with men of any creed, religious or political, if they will obey the law.   My oath of office, my public duty, requires me to be against those who violate it.   [Applause.]

But after all, the foundation of American life is the American home.   That which characterizes and separates us from nations whose political experience and history has been full of strife and discord is the American home, where one mother sits in single, uncrowned honor, the queen of that home.   [Great cheering.]   But, now, my countrymen, I beg to assure you that in every hope you have for Utah, running on these lines, every government on these lines of domestic and social order, I have for every one of you the most cordial greeting, and enter with you, into your most gorgeous hopes.

God bless and keep you all   [People in the audience, "Amen"] and guide you in those safe paths of social purity, of order and peace, that shall make you one of the great commonwealths in the American Union.   [Continued applause.]

GLENWOOD SPRINGS, COLORADO.

MAY 10.

The party was waited upon about 8 o'clock by a committee from Denver, including Gov. Routt, ex-Senator Hill, Mayor Rogers and other citizens and officials, by whom they were assured of a cordial welcome in Denver. Soon afterward the visitors were welcomed formally by Mayor Rogers, of Glenwood Springs. The President, Postmaster General Wanamaker and Mrs. Mc-Kee afterward attended divine services at the First Presbyterian church and heard an eloquent sermon by the pastor, Rev. Dr. Rudolph.

During the afternoon the President received the delegations from Leadville, Aspen, Colorado Springs, and elsewhere. The delegation from Aspen presented him with an elegant souvenir, a beautiful plush case containing, in letters of sterling silver wire, the words, "Free coinage—Aspen silver—Colorado. Honest money. Souvenirs were also presented to the President by the citizens of Glenwood and the Glenwood Board of Trade. A childrens' mass meeting was held at Durand's Opera House at 3 o'clock in honor of the visitors, and it was attended by an immense crowd. Rev. H. M. Law presided, and after the usual devotional exercises Mayor Rogers introduced the President and the Postmaster General, each of whom made short addresses.

The President's address was as follows:

Mr. Mayor, Fellow Citizens and Children:—Our stop
at Glenwood Springs was, as you all know, intended to
be for rest, and yet I have not felt I could deny myself
to this large body of friends assembled from the homes
of this city, and perhaps to an even larger body of friends
who have come from some of the neighboring towns to
pay their respects and testify their good will. The trip
we have been making has been a prolonged one, and it
has been a continued experience of speech-making and
hand-shaking, hence the physical labor has been very
great, and I think if one had been called upon to do the
same amount of work without the stimulous and inspiration which have come from the happy faces and kind
hearts of the people who have greeted us, that almost
any man would have given out. Certainly I would, had
I not been borne up and helped by the wonderful kindness of our people. I have been intensely interested in
what I have seen. It has testified to me of the unity of
the people East and West. Out here you take on some
peculiarities as we do in Indiana, but underneath these
peculiarities there is the same true American grit and
spirit. [Applause.]

It is not wonderful that this should be so. It is not
a mere likeness between different people, because you
are precisely the same people I have known in the Central and Eastern States. Everywhere I have gone I have
seen Hoosiers; everywhere Mr. Wanamaker has gone

he has seen Pennsylvanians; everywhere Gen. Rusk has gone Wisconsin hands has been reached up to him. The new States have been filled up by the enterprising and pushing young men of the older States. They have set out to find here greater advantages, more rapid pathways to wealth and competence. Many of them have found it, many of them are still perhaps in the hard struggle of life; but to all, to every man, whether he is mine owner or handles the pick, I bring you my warmest sympathy and my most sincere thanks for your friendly greeting. [Applause.]

Our Government was instituted by wise men, men of broad views; it was based upon the idea of the equal rights of men; it absolutely rejects the idea of class dis-. tinction, and insists that men should be judged by their behavior. That is a good rule; those who are law-abiding and well disposed, those who pursue their avocations lawfully and with due respect to the rights of others are the true American citizens. [Applause.] I am glad to know that the love of our institutions is so deeply imbedded in your hearts. It has been a most delightful and cheering thing to see that the starry banner, the same old flag that was carried amid the smoke of battle, the rattle of musketry, booming of cannon and the dying of men, is in the hands of such children. [Applause.] Some of the prettiest as well as some of the most hopeful sights we have looked upon have been these companies of children gathered on the streets and hillsides

waving this banner. The American institutions deserve
our watchful care. All our communities should be careful in the beginning to establish law and to maintain it.
It is very difficult, when lawlessness once obtains the
upper hand, to put it down. It is very easy to keep it
out of any community if the well-disposed, true-hearted
people will sink all their differences, religious and political, and stand together as citizens for the good of their
municipality. [Applause.]

I want to thank these children who have gathered
for this Sabbath day's observance. I have had a life that
has been full of labor. From my early manhood until
this hour my time has had many demands upon it. I
have been under the pressure of the practice of my pro-
fession. I have been under the pressure of political
campaigns and of public office, and yet in all these pursuits and under all these conditions I have found simply,
as a physical question without a reference to its religious
aspects at all, that I could do more work by working six
days than seven. [Applause.] I think you will all find
it so, and that as a civil institution rest on the Sabbath
day is good for man. It is not only good, but it is right
of the workingman. [Applause.] Men should have one
free day in which to think of their families, of themselves,
of things that are not material, but are spiritual. [Ap-
plause.]

I desire to express from a sincere and earnest heart
my thanks to you all for all your kindness, giving you

in return simply the pledge that I will in all things keep in mind what seems to me to be the true interests of our people. [Applause.] I have no thought of sections. I have no thought upon any of those great public questions that does not embrace the rights and interests of all our people, and all our States. [Applause.] I believe we shall find a common interest and safe ground upon all these great questions, and by moderating our own views and making reasonable and just concessions, we shall find them all settled wisely, and in the true interest of the people. [Applause.]

LEADVILLE, COLORADO.

MAY 11.

Ten thousand flags were waving in the clear, bracing morning atmosphere, fluttering forth the welcome of the greatest mining camp on earth, as Benjamin Harrison, president of the United States, stepped from his special train and put foot, for the first time, on the crest of the continent. The sun was shining brightly, and as its rays fell upon the snow-capped peaks of the continental range, glistening like diamonds in a veritable sea of silver, a landscape was presented to the presidential party, the like of which had never been seen by any of them before. And as the ringing cheers, mingled with the blowing of whistles, greeted the chief executive as he walked across the Denver and Rio Grande depot to the carriage, he realized that his reception came from the hearts of the people.

From the time the procession started from the depot until it returned, something new was always attracting the attention of the President or some member of the party, and the streamers placed across the avenue, with the amount of money extracted from the hills in the past ten years, the amount paid out in wages for the same length of time, and the profit made by the government, impressed our distinguished visitors with the fact that Leadville was entitled to the proud distinction of being called the "greatest mining camp on earth."

From the balcony of the Hotel Kitchen, the President was introduced by Judge L. M. Goddard and spoke as follows :

My Fellow Citizens: This scene this morning is one that should inspire the dullest heart. This rare, pure atmosphere; this bright sunshine; these colors; this multitude, lifting smiling faces to greet us, is a scene that should lift the dullest heart to emotions of thankfulness and pride, pride wholly separated from personal considerations, and pride that is swelled up by the contemplation that all this is the outcome, the manifestation, the culmination of free American institutions. [Applause.]

We stand here to-day on this mountain top, and see what I think is the highest evidence of American pluck to be found in the United States. [Applause.] I have addressed my fellow citizens on many thousand occasions, but I have never stood before so near the dome. [Applause.] It is a wonderful testimony to the energy and adaptation of the American, that he should have pushed his way to this high altitude, above the snow line, and created these magnificent and extensive industries, and these beautiful and happy homes. I rejoice with you in all that has been accomplished here. I bring thanks to you for that great contribution which you have made to the wealth of the country we all love. I bring to you the assurance that, as an individual citizen and as a public officer, my interest, and my affection, and my duty embraces all the people of this land. You have not got above the high reach of our affections and of our consideration.

I am glad to know that we have, happily, in the past history of our country, in its legislation, found that happy unity of interest which has benificiently affected all our industries, all our people.   We find local interests, and out of them with due regard to them all, we find that happy medium, that general legislation which touches with kindly fingers the humblest homes in all our land.

I do most sincerely thank you for this token of the product of your mines.   It is a precious metal, but much more precious to me is the kindly thought of the generous welcome which you have given us in Leadville here to-day.

This rare and stimulating atmosphere my lungs are unaccustomed to, and you will permit me to close these remarks by wishing for you all—for the men who, deep down in these mines, are toilsomely working out these precious metals; for those who welcome you in your homes when you return from your toil, the wives and children who add grace and sweetness to your lives, to these children who have gathered to meet us, we give you a most cordial salutation and a regretful good-bye.

PUEBLO, COLORADO.

MAY 11.

Pueblo people turned out almost unanimously to welcome the chief magistrate of the nation, and nowhere with more genuine cordiality and enthusiasm was he greeted than in the great smelting center of the West.

The entire presidential party were driven over the city, escorted by the local military and civic societies. Nearly 8,000 children were massed on the public square and were addressed as follows by the President:

Children of the public schools and others, I am glad to meet such an immense number here, and I can't allow this opportunity to pass without expressing to you my thanks for this welcome.

Riding to the depot the President was introduced to the vast multitude by Col. I. W. Stanton and delivered the following address:

Mr. Mayor and Fellow Citizens: The brief time which we were able, in this hasty journey, to allot to the city of Pueblo has now almost expired. It has given me great pleasure to ride through the streets of this enterprising and prosperous municipality. It has given me pleasure to see that you are concentrating here very important business interests, which must in the future make you a very important commercial center in this great State of Colorado. [Cheers.] You have in this country a variety of resources unexcelled, I think, by any other State. [Cheers.] It is quite natural that interest was first directed towards the precious metals—the mining of silver and gold—and that commoner things

should have been for the time overlooked. The mining
camp was the beginning, and nowhere in all our history
has capacity for organization, for the proper framing of
the necessary laws to secure order been so perfectly demonstrated as in the mining camps of the West. [Ap-
plause.] Coming here entirely beyond the range of civil
institutions, whose clerks, sheriffs and public officers
could not give their aid to suppress the unruly, coming
here at a time when our national mining laws were un-
framed, these pioneer miners of Colorado, Nevada, Montana, and Idaho wrought for themselves in these mining
camps a system of government and a fair system of
mining laws that has received the approval of the government. [Applause.] You are coming now to realize
that in the baser metals, as we call them, with which
your great hills are stored, as iron, there lie means of
development. This is an iron age. With these modern
inventions for converting iron cheaply into steel, with
the disappearance or scarcity of the timber, with which
our fathers built, the manufacture of structural iron to
enter into our great buildings, both commercial and public, has developed a marvelous industry in this country.
I do not doubt that these smelters of the precious metals,
this rolling mill, to which reference has been made, is
the foundation of increases in all such establishments to
give employment to increasing numbers of laborers, to
whom we will pay full, honest American wages. [Loud
cheers.] You are also turning your attention to the de-

velopment of your horticultural and agricultural resources. You were content at first to pack in your flour and meal and pork on bronchos, over these wild prairies and steep passes. You have now found that many of those valleys, touched by the mystical hands of irrigation, are capable of producing not only staple crops but fruits and flowers to delight the heart of man. [Applause.] We passed this morning through a region where I was surprised to see orchards that reminded me of California. Now, for all these things, for the beneficent influences under which you enjoy them, for that kind law that has distributed these public domains freely to every man who desired to make a home for himself and his family, for free government that extends its protection over the humble as well as the mighty, for all these resources of sky and air and earth the people of Colorado should be joyously thankful. [Loud cheers.] I am glad to hail you as fellow citizens. I am glad for a moment to stand in your midst—to see these great resources and to assure you that my heart is with you in the development of them all—[cheers]—and I am glad to know that Colorado, this young Centennial State, has established a system of free public schools unexcelled by any State in the Union. [Cheers.] But, my friends, as I said before, I am in slavery to the railroad schedule and time is up. Good-bye.

COLORADO SPRINGS, COLORADO.

MAY 11.

An immense concourse of people were gathered at the depot to greet the distinguished visitors, and it was with difficulty that the police-men could clear and keep clear the depot platform and grounds, and form the line of march of carriages, military companies and organizations. The entire line of travel, from the depot to the Garfield school, was thronged with people, who gave a hearty welcome to the party as it passed.

On reaching the school a beautiful scene was presented, and one which must have given the President great pleasure. The large yard and the street was filled with children, the number being estimated at 1,500. The President arose in his carriage and said :

My Friends: You have very appropriately named this school in which you have gathered a portion of the children of Colorado Springs for instruction. I understand another of your public schools is named after Abraham Lincoln. That too is a most appropriate designation, for where in all the story of our country among its men who have been illustrious in civil pursuits or in war can two names be found which furnish more inspiration and hope to the youth of the land than the names of Lincoln and Garfield? [Applause.] Both men came of parentage so poor that no advantages attended their early years; and yet, each by his own inherent energy and indomitable will, by the perservering improvement of the meagre opportunities he enjoyed, reached the highest place in our land and are now embalmed in the affectionate recollection of their countrymen. I bid you all to read the lessons of these great lives, and to ponder them well; for, while not all may achieve all they achieved, useful and honorable positions in life may be achieved by you all. Wishing you every prosperity and success, I bid you all good bye. [Cheers.]

From the balcony of The Antlers hotel Mayor Sprague gave the address of welcome, to which the president responded as follows:

Mr. Mayor and Fellow Citizens: I am sure you will crown the kindness which you have shown me to-day by permitting me to make my response to these words of welcome exceedingly brief. I have spoken already four or five times to-day. The chilly evening air will not allow me to exercise my voice with the customary immunity, but I cannot refrain from saying to you how much we have been pleased by the hasty glimpse we have been permitted to have of this beautiful city. The fame of

Colorado Springs has spread throughout the entire East.

Much I had heard of the beauty of its location, the grandeur and sublimity of its mountain, of the health-giving atmosphere which fills these valleys, and of its marvelous springs, refreshing and life-giving, which break from your mountain side; of these marvelous and weird products of time that stand in the Garden of the Gods—of all these I have heard.

I regret that the brevity of our stay is such that we shall not be able to see and enjoy this, but, my countrymen, no spring that ever broke from mountain side, no bracing air that ever filled these valleys, was more refreshing and invigorating to the invalid, or to the weary than your hearty greeting here has been to us. .[Applause.]

I visit your great State for the first time. When this journey has been completed, only two of the States of the Union, and only its most distant territory will have escaped my personal inspection and observation. From Maine to California, from the line of Michigan, where it is hid by the waters of the Sault Ste. Marie, to the Savannah, I have crossed this broad land of ours, and, out of all this journeying, out of all this mingling with our people, I have come to be a better American.

We have a country whose diversity of climate and soil and production, makes it in a degree not true of any other people in the world, independent and self-contained. We have our philanthropic symphathies for mankind

the world around, but we could live very comfortably if
there was no other country in the world except this.
[Applause.] None of the necessities of life, and few of
the luxuries would be denied to us, if we should limit
ourselves to articles of American growth and product.
[Applause.]

But, better than all this, greater than all our material
production, are those things that enter into and characterize the American social and political life. A distinguished Englishman, journeying in this country not
many years ago, speaking of his observations, rather
caustically mentioned that the question most often asked
him was whether he was not surprised by the great strides
of this country. He was a man of discernment, one
who looked beneath the surface, who said that greater
still, to him, was the surprise that over sixty millions of
people would maintain and preserve, under free republican institutions, the social order, the individual liberty
which was maintained here. Greater still, was the marvel that this great people could have survived and maintained its institutions under the terrible strain of the
great civil war. Greater than all else was the unification
of the people which followed that period; and so, my
countrymen, we are to-day truly one great people.

We have a government whose concern it is to let the
people alone, to work out freely with those agencies and
powers that God has given them, each one his own individual destiny and career.

I rejoice to be with you to-night as an American citizen. I rejoice in the glory which the century has brought, and which, ere the close of this century, will be greatly enhanced; but above all local pride, I rejoice to-night that we are citizens of one ¡country, knowing one flag, one constitution, one common purpose—to work out one destiny for this whole land.   [Great applause.]

DENVER, COLORADO.
MAY 12.

President Harrison has been in our fair city and spent a day here, and has gone on his journey back to the seat of government.   The reception was worthy of him, worthy of his record as a brave and true soldier and as an able and conscientious senator, worthy of his great position as chief of this nation, and worthy of his able and honest and pure administration.

The reception was also becoming for Denver. It was fitting to her greatness, her wealth, her enterprise, her ambition, her hopes.   It was also, in some ways, a reception by the State. Cities of Western and Southern Colorado had before, indeed, done all honor to the Chief Magistrate of the nation. They had made cheering, inspiring manifestations of their patriotic and national feeling. But Denver is the capital of the young commonwealth. Here had gathered thousands of people from the towns and cities through which the presidential train was not to pass and could not pass.

Probably 20,000 people were assembled in the capital grounds to here the President speak. After the speeches by Gov. Routt and Mayor Rogues, the President spoke as follows:

Governor Routt, Mr. Mayor, Pioneers of Colorado, Comrades of the Grand army of the Republic and Fellow Citizens:—This scene is inspiring. This beautiful city, the fame of which your journeying citizens have not failed to carry to the far East [laughter and cheers] had become known to me, as we can know by the hearing of the ear; and I am rejoiced to add to my pleasant impressions of Colorado and of its commercial and political capital this sight of the eye, which has but deepened and enlarged the favorable impressions which I brought to your State. It is a marvelous thing that we are here in a State whose existence dates from the dawn of the second century of our national life.

What a tremendous testimony to the organizing power and energy of the American people this great

State is. [Cheers.] That these wastes, so unpromising
to the eye in that early time, should have been invaded
by the restless energy of the indomitable men; that they
should have seen in visions that which was to follow
their heroic efforts for the development of these hidden
resources; that no drouth or drifting sand, no threat of
mountain or of sky could turn back these brave hearts
who had set their faces to pierce and uncover the hidden
riches of these mountains. [Cheers.]

The pioneers of Colorado are worthy of honor. Those
who have not entered into their labors, who have
come not toilsomely but upon swift and easy wings into
the heritage that they have opened, should always and
everywhere gratefully acknowledge the services of those
who made this easy pathway for their feet. [Cheers.]

Your State is blessed in the diversity of its resources.
You do not depend upon any one of the great industries
of civilized life. You have taken from your mines stores
of the precious metals; but when these are gone, or their
supply is diminished, you will turn your eyes toward
those metals that we call base, but that, after all, enter
in so many ways into human life that they supply more
enduring, and, in the end, more profitable industries.

Your iron and coal and lead and building stone will
be sources of income, inexhaustible. These valleys,
touched by the magical power of irrigation, will yield to
your population abundant food, and you will yet have
within yourselves that happy commercial condition of a

State producing and exchanging within its own limits nearly all the necessaries of life. [Cheers.] Transportation is always a burden. The industrial condition is always best when the producer and consumer are near together.

I am glad to know that you have not been so busy in delving into the earth; you have not so much turned your minds to precious metal as to have forgotten that there is a blue above you; that there are aspirations and hopes and glories that are greater than all material things. [Cheers.]

You have not failed to make sure, that the children, the blessed children of your household that are now coming on, are made secure in the possession of a well ordered and well endowed common school system. [Cheers.] What a testimony it is to the American character that, however intense the push for the things of this life, however eager the pursuit of gain, you can never assemble a community of two hundred people that they do not begin to organize schools for the children. [Cheers,]

These common schools are not simply nurseries of intellectual training; they are nurseries of citizenship. [Cheers.] It has been a most happy sight to see the old banner that we bore into the smoke of battle and carried over dying comrades to place it in triumph on the ramparts of the enemy, now in the hands of all the children of Colorado. [Cheers.] Proof has been made a thousand times, proof will be made whenever the occasion arises, that, much as we pursue gain and personal ends, we have nothing—property, life—that we do not freely lay down upon the alter of our country and the general good. [Cheers.] But, my fellow citizens, this assemblage is too vast and the demand upon my time for public speech has been too protracted to enable me to pursue these remarks further.

Comrades of the Grand Army of the Republic, survivors of the great war, whose success preserved all that our fathers had devised and established; whose success brought back this flag in honor and established it again, the undisputed emblem of an indissoluble Union; [cheers] God hath bountifully lengthened out your days that you might have some glimpse of the glory that has come from the achievements in which you bore an honorable part. But only the vision of the prophet, reaching out over all time to come, can catch the full glory of what your deeds have wrought. I give you to-day a most affectionate greeting. [Cries of "God bless you."] I give you a regretful good-by.

May you hold in the community where you live that respect and honor to which you are entitled. Let no Grand Army man ever dishonor in civil life the noble record he made in the war. [Cheers.] May every blessing follow you; and, if it shall not be in God's dispensation to give you riches, at least, comrades, you shall die with the glorious satisfaction of having contributed to the greatest work that man ever wrought for humanity and

God; and wrapped in the flag you followed, your comrades will one by one see that in honored graves your bodies rest until the resurrection, and that on each returning day of decoration, flowers are strewn upon your graves.

Citizens of Denver, I cannot close without expressing the great satisfaction and suprise with which I have witnessed this morning the magnificent commercial development which has been made here. These streets, these towering, substantial and stately houses in which your commerce is transacted, place you, in enterprise and in the beauty of your streets, among the greatest cities of the land. I do not think any city so young can claim so high a place. [Cheers.]

I thank you very sincerely for a demonstration which I cannot accept as personal—all this is too great for any man, but as a spontaneous tribute to our free institution. I accept this as an evidence that in all essential things we are one people.

The fuller revelation of that fact to us all has been worth all the labor and time we have mutually expended in this long journey. In all essential things we are one; we divide and strive and debate, but we are patriotic American citizens, having a love for the constitution and the flag that brings us all at last to submit our opinions to the lawfully expressed wish of the majority. [Cheers.] And now again good-by. I shall leave behind me every good wish for your prosperity individually, municipality and as a State. [Cheers.]

HASTINGS, NEBRASKA.

MAY 13.

The presidential party received a royal welcome. The streets leading to the Burlington depot were jammed with people from the city and contiguous points. The railroad yards were so packed with humanity that it was with considerable difficulty that the trains were moved.

James N. Clarke, in the absence of Mayor Clarke introduced the president.

Mr. Harrison spoke substantially thus:

My Fellow Countrymen: There is a freshness and a beauty about the Nebraska prairies, but I hope I will not fall in your esteem if I say I do not like to get up early. [Shouts, "Neither do we."] Occasionally, in our trip, we seem to pick up an hour. When I retired at Denver last night, at none too early an hour, I was told we would be at Hastings at 6:20. But we arrived here, it seems to me, at 5:20 by the time I went to bed by last night. But my friends, all these things that make labor of travel are as nothing compared with the great gratification which we find in such assemblages as this.

We have seen the arid land where the water ran in ditches and did not fall in showers. Travel has its advantages and its disadvantages, but I must confess that

it seems more homelike for me to get back to the land
where the showers fall and everything is fresh and green.
There is a great diversity of mineral and agricultural
products found in the United States. The Creator did
not make all alike. The diversity is found everywhere
in production. It is found in the field and crop, but
never in the people. We are one people. [Applause.]
The people I have met in California and Arizona are substantially the same as those here. There are Yankees
here, and people from Pennsylvania, and Wisconsin, and
I think the Ohio man must be here, [shouts, "here we
are.] and the Hoosier, too; but we are all the same people.
The westerners are the overspill of the enterprising east.
They keep going a little farther west, a little farther west,
until they reach at last the Pacific. But throughout all there
is the same love for the one flag. We have not paused
at any little way station and been surrounded by a crowd
of persons gathered together to greet us but some one
with the American flag was there, and an American
cheer for it. [Applause.] Sometimes the incidents were
almost pathetic. At one little way station in Arizona, as
we drew up in the darkness, there were a half a dozen
ranchers there on the platform. I noticed on the lapels
of two or three coats the Grand Army button. One of
them shouted: "There are but few of us, but let's give a
cheer for the old flag, boys."

I thank you most cordially for your gathering here.
I do not know whether it is prejudice or not, but anyway

I always have a very high opinion of a State whose chief production is corn.   [Laughter and applause.]

OMAHA, NEBRASKA.

MAY 13.

Nowhere was the President received by a heartier or more enthusiastic welcome than was accorded him by the citizens of Omaha.   The people turned out en masse in honor of the occasion, and they cheered the President nearly the entire time of his appearance in the city in public.

The visitors were met at the station by a large committee of citizens, headed by Mayor Cushing and the City Council, and taken to the court house stand.   Their escort was composed of mounted police, the 2d Regiment United States Infantry, Gen. Wheaton commanding, and the Omaha Guards, who acted as a special guard of honor to the President.

Mayor Cushing made a short address of welcome, and, in closing, introduced the President, who advanced to the front of the stand, amid great enthusiasm and delivered the following speech:

Fellow Citizens: I cannot accept without feeling the deepest gratitude for these cordial words of welcome in behalf of the people of this great city. Twice before it has been my pleasure to spend a brief time in this great commercial metropolis of the valley of the Missouri. I have had an opportunity, therefore, to witness the development which your city has made. I recollect it as I saw it in 1881, and as I see it to-day I feel that I need to be told where I am. [Applause.]

These mighty structures dedicated to commerce, these majestic churches lifting their spires toward heaven, these majestic school houses consecrated to those who shall in the future stand in our places and assume the responsibility of your public institutions, these great stock yards where the meat is produced, which is raised by the great Missouri valley, these thousands of happy homes—all characterize your great city. It is a marvel, a tribute to the enterprise and power of the American people, and is unsurpassed by any city in the United States.

I am glad as I turn my face toward Washington, as I hasten to take up my public duties, partially put aside during the journey—I rejoice to receive here in Omaha that kindly feeling with which we were welcomed through the South to the Pacific coast. If anything need to call for a perfect surrender of all personal feeling that is an absolute consecration of the pride of the people, I have found it in all their demonstrations. I shall

always have it.   It is the characteristic of a free people.
We need parties, debate, politics, yet it is a pleasure to
notice how large a stock of common patriotism I find in
all the people you have here in Nebraska, this State of
majestic capabilities.

I have seen orange groves and all fruits which enrich
and characterize California.   I have seen their summit
cities.   I have seen mining camps on the peaks, where
men delve into the earth and bring out the riches stored
there, but I return again to the land of the corn stalk
with an affection I can't understand.   I am sure these
friends who have delighted us with visions of lovliness
and prosperity, will excuse me if my birth and raising in
Ohio and Indiana leads me, to the conclusion that
the States where they raise corn are the greatest on
earth.   We have a surplus in this great valley for which
we must seek foreign markets.   I am pleased to know
that 90 per cent or more of our agricultural products are
consumed by our own people.   I do not know how soon,
but we shall I think, cease to be dependent on foreign
markets for farm products.

With the rapid development of manufactures, with
the rapid occupation of the public domain, brings to
mind that with the increase in agriculture, it cannot be
a distant day until the farmer will realize his ideal, a
market out of his own wagon for his products.

It has been a source of constant thought and zealous
effort on the part of the administration at Washington to

secure larger foreign markets for our farm products. In
the last two years many hinderances to the marketing of
our meat production have been removed. I rejoice to
know we have now freer access to England and Europe
than in many years. I rejoice to see that this brought
better prices to stock raisers in the western valleys. I
believe under the provisions of reciprocal trade we shall
open a great, larger and nearer market for the products
of the Nebraska farm. So distant are you from the Atlantic seaboard it may seem to you that we do not look
after your interest in the marine trade. The re-estab-
lishment of the American merchant marine may not be
perceptible to you. Not long ago I made an investigation of the cargo of a Brazilian steamer from New York.
Twenty-five States contributed to that cargo, and among
those States was Nebraska. And so by such methods as
we can it is our purpose to enlarge our foreign markets
for our great country. We hope and trust, as does the
great west and east, that when this commerce is founded
on the sea it shall be carried in American bottoms.
While at San Francisco I saw three great ships enter the
Golden Gate. One carried the flag of Hawaii, and two
the flags of England. At Portland they took pains to
tow up from the lower harbor an American ship and
deck it in bunting. I was a curious sight, and one they
thought important to show the visiting strangers.

I hope the day is not far distant when the sight of
great American ships with the stars and stripes floating

at their peaks will be not only in our ports, but in all the busy marts of the world.

This government of ours can develop trade for everybody. Its theory is largely individual liberty, and to take out of the way of legislation what obstructs the free, honest pursuit of human industries, and to allow each individual to have the best possible chance to develop the highest prosperity for himself and family. It must provide a currency. I believe we will not consent to return to the old system of issuing money to State banks. I only desire to say this on common ground. Whatever money we have, paper or currency, we want good money. I have an idea that every dollar issued should be as good as any dollar we issue, for whenever we issue a paper or coin dollar that is not worth a dollar its first errand is to pay a workingman or farmer for a day's toil. No one should have an honest dollar before a laborer or farmer.

But, my countrymen, I had not intended to speak so long. I am not here as a partisan, but as an American citizen desiring to enhance the prosperity of all our people, to have this great government in all it undertakes to touch with an equal hand the rich and poor alike.

Nothing has been so impressive in all this journey as the magnificent patriotism I have seen. I have seen enough American flags to wrap the world around. School children have waved it to me and many times in lonesome country homes on the bleak sands a man, a

woman or a boy would open a cabin door and wave the
starry banner in greeting at our train. I am sure the
same magnificent patriotism and American spirit pre-
vades you all. God bless you all; may you prosper in
everything you undertake and may prosperity and increase come to your city and give it security, social order
and obedience to law.

There was but one " hitch " in the entire
programme and that was at the high school
grounds. The 12,000 school children were
gathered on the west of the big building where
a platform had been erected for the President.
On the east of the building a crowd of 10,000
adults had gathered, and there the President's
carriage was stopped. Mr. Harrison arose to
his feet and made a two-minute speech which
was intended for the children. At the conclusion of his remarks he was apprised of the mistake and instantly had the driver rein in his
steeds, and alighting with his escort he made his
way through the clamoring crowd and mounted
the platform and said:

My little friends:—You do not feel half so badly as I
do at the thought that I made a mistake and made the

speech I intended for you to your papas and mammas. I have not the time to attempt to repeat it, but I cannot get away without telling you of the affectionate interest I have in all the children of this great country. Bless you—you are the blossoms of our homes. With a good-by, another God bless you, and I am off.

MISSOURI HOSPITALITY EXTENDED.

Governor Francis sent the subjoined telegrams to President Harrison:

JEFFERSON CITY, MO., May 12.—To Hon. Benjamin Harrison, Denver, Colo.: The people of Missouri, as well as myself, would feel honored if you could arrange to spend at least a few hours at the State capitol, where I should be pleased to entertain you as my guest. I observe from the public prints that you will pass through Missouri enroute home. If you cannot come to Jefferson, please advise me what stops, if any, you will make in the State. The citizens of Maryville, a flourishing city on your itinerary through Northwest Missouri, are very desirious that you stop with them an hour or more, and I earnestly second their request.

(Signed.)   DAVID R. FRANCIS, Governor.

JEFFERSON CITY, MO., May 13, 1891.—Hon. Benjamin Harrison, care Mayor Green, Maryville, Mo.: Impossible for me to meet you at Maryville after receipt to-day of answer to my telegram advising of your ten-minutes' stop there to-night. That city will express its appreciation of the honor. Missouri welcomes you to her borders and her people regret that your stay among them is not longer, to the end that you might have a better opportunity to know the advantages and resources of this most highly favored member of the republic over whose destinies you preside, and in order that they might make manifestation of the esteem in which they hold the President of the United States. I conclude you will make no other stop in Missouri.

(Signed)   DAVID R. FRANCIS, Governor.

HANNIBAL, MISSOURI.

MAY 14.

As the first rays of bright spring sun shown on the seven hills of Hannibal, Mo., the presidential special arrived at that city in the midst of blowing of whistles and the shouts of thousands. The President addressed the multitude as follows:

My Fellow Citizens:—I have only time to assure you that I appreciate very highly this evidence of your respect. We have extended our journey to the Pacific coast; we have crossed the sandy plain, where for days together the eye saw little to refresh it, where the green of the blue-grass, which is so restful to the eye, was wanting, and yet again and again at some lone station in the desert a few children from a school, and some of the enterprising people who had pushed out there to make new homes, assembled with this old banner in their hands and gave us a hearty American welcome. I am glad to return to this central body of states in which I was raised; glad to be again in the land of the buckeye, the beech and the maple. To these dear children I want to say one word of thanks. They have done for us much on this journey to make it pleasant; their bright faces have cheered us; I love to see them. The care the states are taking for their education is wisely bestowed. God bless them all; open to their feet pleasant ways and qualify them better than we have been in our generation, to uphold and perpetuate these magnificent civil institutiocs. Thanking you most sincerely for this kindly demonstration I bid you good-bye. [Great cheers.]

SPRINGFIELD, ILLINOIS.

MAY 14.

The President and party had an ovation here. Their arrival was heralded by the firing of a national salute and the cheering of an immense crowd. Governor Fifer, Mayor Lawrence, Senators Cullom and Palmer, Representatives Springer and Henderson, Collector John M. Clark of Chicago, ex-Governor Oglesby and Col. E. D. Swain were among the first to greet the visitors and bid them welcome to the capitol of the State. The local militia, Grand Army men and civic organizations were drawn up in line at the station, and escorted the party through gayly decorated streets, past the State capital, to the Lincoln monument in Oak Ridge cemetery, where the formal ceremonies took place.

Mayor Lawrence presided and Governor Fifer delivered an eloquent address of welcome to which the President responded as follows:

Governor Fifer and Fellow Citizens: During this extended journey, in the course of which we have swept from the Atlantic coast to the Golden Gate, and northward to the limits of our territory, we have stood in many spots of interest and looked upon scenes that were full of historical associations, and of national interest and inspiration. The interest of this journey culminates today as we stand here for a few moments about the tomb of Lincoln. As I passed through the Southern States

and noticed those great centers of busy industry which
have been builded since the war; as I saw how the fires
of furnaces had been kindled where there was once a
solitude, I could not then but think and say it was the
hand that now lies beneath these stones that kindled and
inspired all that we beheld; all these fires of industry
were lighted at the funeral pyre of slavery. The proclamation of Abraham Lincoln can be read on all those
mountain sides where free men are now bending their
energies to the development of States that had long been
under the paralysis of human slavery.

I come to-day to this consecrated and sacred spot with
a heart filled with emotions of gratitude that God
who wisely turned towards our Eastern shores a body of
God-fearing and liberty-loving men to found this Republic did not fail to find for us in the hour of our extrem-
ity, one who was competent to lead the hearts and sympathies, and hold up the courage of our people in the time
of our greatest national peril.

The life of Abraham Lincoln teaches more useful
lessons than any other character in American history.
Washington stands remote from us. We think of him
as dignified and reserved, but we think of Lincoln as
one whose tender touch the children, the poor—all classes
of our people—felt at their firesides and loved. The love
of our people is drawn to him because he had such a
great heart—such a human heart. The asperities and
hardships of his early life did not dull, but broadened

and enlivened his sympathies. That sense of justice, that love of human liberty which dominated all his life, is another characteristic which our people will always love.

You have here in keeping a most precious trust. Toward this spot the feet of the reverend patriots of the years to come will bend their way. As the story of Lincoln's life is read, his virtues will mold and inspire many lives. I have studied it and been filled with wonder and admiration. His life was an American product; no other soil could have produced it. The greatness of it has not yet been fully discovered or measured. As the inner history of the times in which he lived is written, we find how his great mind turned and moved, in time of peril and delicacy, the affairs of our country in their home and foreign relations with that marvelous tact, with that never-failing common sense which characterized this man of the people. And that impressive lesson we have this morning. I see in the military uniform of our country, standing as guards about this tomb, the souls of a race that had been condemned to slavery and was emancipated by his immortal proclamation. And what an appropriate thing it is that these whose civil rights were curtailed even in this State are now the trusted, affectionate guards of the tomb in which he sleeps.

We will all again and again read the story of Lincoln's life and will find our hearts and minds enlarged, our loves and our charities broadened and our devotion

to the Constitution, the flag and the free government
which he preserved to us intensified. And now, my
friends, most cordially do I thank you for these kind
words of welcome. I shall go from this tomb impressed
with new thoughts as to the responsibilities of those who
bear the responsibilities, though in less troublous times,
of that great man to whose memory my soul bows this
morning. [Applause.]

When the President closed he was presented
by Governor Fifer on behalf of citizens of Peters-
burg, Ill., with a gold headed cane made from
the Lincoln store building at New Salem. The
President made a short address from his carriage at the station. He said :

The demand for my presence in Washington is such
that I cannot protract my stay with you here this morning. I beg all to believe that most heartily and sincerely I thank you for this cordial welcome from Illinois; for
the interesting moments that we have spent about the
tomb of that man who would have made the fame of
Illinois imperishable and Springfield a mecca for patriotic feet if not another man in the history of the State
had come to eminence—Abraham Lincoln. [Cheers.] In
his life you have a treasury of instruction for your children, a spring of inspiration for your people that will be
lasting. [Cheers.]

DECATUR, ILLINOIS.

MAY 14.

Fully 7,000 people gathered at the depot to greet the presidential party, and after a brief address of welcome by Mayor Chambers the President spoke as follows:

Mr. Mayor and Fellow Citizens:—We have been now something more than four weeks traversing this broad and beautiful domain which, without regard to state line we call our country. We have passed with such rapidity that our intercourse with the people has necessarily been brief and attended by many inconveniences to them. Everything that kind hearts could do to make the trip pleasant to us has been done, and yet I have always felt that our hasty call at these prosperous cities where so much pains have been taken in decoration to do honor to us, gives us opportunity to make very inadequate returns to them. We have been shooting like a meteor as to rapidity, but without its luminosity. [Laughter.] It is very pleasant again after seeing California, Arizona, Idaho and Colorado, states in which the annual rainfall is inadequate to the annual crops, and where the dependence of the husbandman is wholly upon irrigation, to come again in these central states, familiar to me from my boyhood, to see crops that the Lord waters in every season. The land of the bluegrass is the land of my love. Nowhere can there be seen fairer landscapes, nowhere richer farms, than here in your own great state of Illinois, a state whose history has been full of illustrious achievments, rich in possibilities, where lived our illustrious sons; a state whose population is intelligent, contented, orderly and liberty loving; a state whose development has not yet begun to approach its possible limits; a state having advantages by the location, swept as it is by two of the great water ways of the continent, advantages of access and markets by lake and rail and river, unexcelled by any other State in the Union; a state that has not forgotten that the permanence of our free institutions depends upon the in telligence of the people, and has carefully, at the very beginning, laid a foundation for a common school system in which every man's child may have a free education. [Cheers.]   These are not simply schools of intelligence, but as I have said before, they are schools of statesmanship.   They tend as much as any other public institution to make our people a nation loving people. Here on these benches and on this playground the people of rich and poor mingle together, and the pampered son gets his airs rubbed off with the vigor of his playmates.   ["That's so," and cheers.]   Our government does not undertake to regulate many of the affairs of civil life.   The bright blue sky of hope is above every boy's head, affording great opportunities for advancement, and then our people are left to themselves.   Certain great duties are devolved upon the government—to provide revenue and finance and in every branch of public interest to legislate in the general interests of all the people. I thank you most heartily for this great demonstration. We leave you with our thanks, our best wishes for your State, your city, and especially for these dear little ones from your schools who come to greet us. [Applause.]

XENIA, OHIO.

MAY 14.

The Presidential party was greeted by an immense crowd of people, including ladies.

Mayor Howard, Hon. John Little, Postmaster Fulton, Geo. V. Good, president of the city council, and Chas. L. Spencer were on the train with the President. Mayor Howard briefly introduced him. The President said:

My Fellow Citizens: I began my day's work this morning at five o'clock, and I have already spoken ten times, to audiences assembled, as you are here to-night, to give us welcome as we speed across the country. And yet I feel that a few spoken words are but small return to you who have been at the pains to gather here, and now stand about our train to express your friendly regard.

No man can be worthy to administer public office in this free republic of ours who does not sincerely covet the good will and respect of the people. ["That's so," and applause.] It is not possible that we should all agree as to our views of public questions. We are so constituted, so born, so educated that we take different views of the great public questions with which Congress and the Executive have to deal. But it is pleasant to observe, as I have on this long journey I have been taking, that while we have many points of difference we have a great many more of agreement, [applause] and that we are all pursuing, by different means, the same great end —the glory of our country—the permanency of our institutions—the order—social order—of the communities in which we dwell, and the general good of all the people. [Applause.]

This government was devised for all people. Mr. Lincoln very felicitously described it as "a government of the people"—one that sprang from, that was originated by them; a government for the people—administered for their good—having no other end than to promote the greatest good of the greatest number. Now, I am glad to know that we are so thoroughly and heartily in love with our institutions. You are thinking now, perhaps, of the government at Washington; but, my countrymen, the springs of all ˈgood government—the

more important things after all are in your local community. ["That's so."] It is in the township—in the
school district—in the city—the municipality—that the
utmost care needs to be taken. If these affairs are wisely
and economically administered, so that each one of these
small civil divisions is pure in its administration, economical and just in the assessment and distribution of
public burdens, and accomplishes fully the purpose of
civil government, then the aggregate of all these things
that make up the State and National Government is sure
to be right. [Applause.] I trust that we will give due
attention to these things, for it is the aggregate of these
that makes up the prosperity and happiness, and greatness of the community. Social order, decent lives, repression of lawlessness, and the encouragement and
promotion of the public schools, and everything that
tends to security and good order, decent living, good
education, and the right instruction of our children in
these things, we are to find our security and growth as a
nation. Upon these foundation stones our prosperity
rests; and I am glad to know that so much careful
thought is now being given by our public men, and by
our people generally, to these questions. [Applause.]

I thank you for your attendance here, and for your
cordial greeting, and bid you good night. [Cheers.]

INDIANAPOLIS.

A large delegation of Indiana friends met
the President at Montezuma, Ind. He was
overcome by the greeting, and for the first time
since he started from Washington was unable
to respond to the demand for a speech at any
length. He managed to say:

My Friends:—We have had a long journey, and one
that has been attended by a great many pleasant incidents. We had cheers of welcome reaching from our
first stop at Roanoke, Va., stretching across the mountains of Tennessee and Northern Georgia and Alabama,
down through Arkansas and Texas, and along the
Pacific coast. Everywhere we had the most cordial
and kindly greeting : but as I crossed to-day the border
line of Indiana, and meet again these old friends, I find
in your welcome a sweetness that exceeds it all.

At this point the tears came to the President's
eyes, and his utterance became so choked that
he could say no more. He soon recovered, however, and extended a cordial welcome to the
Indianapolis Reception Committee, which then
boarded the train.

When the train arrived at Indianapolis there was a magnificent display of affection by the people, and the President said:

I do not think I can speak much to-day. The strain of the long journey and frequent calls made on me to speak, from Washington to the Golden Gate, and from the far Northwest territory back to Indianapolis have somewhat exhausted me, body and mind, and have made my heart so open to these impressions as I greet my old friends that I can not, I fear, command myself.

Our pathway has been marked by the plaudits of the multitude, our way strewn with flowers. We have journeyed through the orchards of California laden with fruit; we have climbed the summits of great mountains from which rich metals have been extracted, then we have dropped into fruitful valleys, and our whole pathway has been made glad by the friendly acclaim of our American fellow citizens without regard to party. But all the sweetness of these flowers, all the beauty of these almost tropical landscapes, all the richness of these precious mines sink into forgetfulness as I recieve to-day this welcome from my old friends. [There was a perceptible moisture in the President's eyes, and his voice almost failed him.]

My manhood has known no other home but this. It was the scene of my early struggles. It has been the scene and instrument and support of my early success in life. I come to lay down before you to-day my offering of thankfulness for the friendly helpfulness in boyhood and in all hours down to this.

I left you two years ago to take up the work of the most responsible office in the world. I went to these untried duties sustained by your helpful friendliness. I come after two years to confess many errors, but to say to you that I have had but one thought in my mind—to use whatever influence I have for the general good of all the people.

Our stay is so brief that I must deny myself the pleasure of taking all these friends by the hand. God bless you all. I have not forgotten, I can not forget, Indianapolis. I look forward, if my life is spared, to this as the city where I shall rest when the hard toil is done. I love its homes and rejoice in its commercial prosperity. Pardon further speech, and allow me to say God bless you every one, and good-bye.

WASHINGTON, D. C.

MAY 15.

The grand tour of President Harrison and party, which began April 14 last, ended at 5:30 o'clock this afternoon, when the presidential train came to a standstill in the Pennsylvania railroad station here exactly on time. The great journey of 10,000 miles had been accomplished without an accident and without deviation from the pre-arranged schedule, except on one occasion.

Between Washington and Baltimore the members of the party and the employes assembled in the observation car and the President made a short speech, in which he thanked all those who had accompanied him for the courtesies extended. He paid a high compliment to Mr. George W. Boyd, the genial passenger agent of the Pennsylvania railroad, who had charge of the train, for what he had achieved in keeping them exactly to the time schedule.

www.ingramcontent.com/pod-product-compliance
Lightning Source LLC
Chambersburg PA
CBHW030537040726
47497CB00008B/2487